Puffin Books

LOVE ME, LOVE ME NOT

'Love may come from someone who has been just a friend before.'

Maria is always looking out for her neighbour. . . It is love at first sight for Pete when he sees Kate on the train. For each of the kids in Year Eight it is different. Cassie just wants to be kissed, like in the films, and Andrew and Kim are friends, but Cathy and Rodney. . .

Love. You might want to try it – but will it be what you imagine? Find out what happens in this real life collection of stories about the time in your life when memories are made.

Love Me, Love Me Not was shortlisted for the 1994 Australian Children's Book of the Year Award (Older Readers).

'Some people think *Love Me, Love Me Not* is simply a collection of stories, but I read it as a novel tracing the progression of sexual awakening to the first relationships – except that each stage in the process happens to be experienced by a different kid.'

Jenny Pausacker, *The Age*

ALSO BY LIBBY GLEESON

NOVELS

Eleanor, Elizabeth
I am Susannah
Dodger

PICTURE BOOKS

One Sunday
Big Dog
Where's Mum?
Mum Goes to Work
Uncle David
Sleeptime

Libby Gleeson

LOVE ME, LOVE ME NOT

Puffin Books

Puffin Books
Penguin Books Australia Ltd
487 Maroondah Highway, PO Box 257
Ringwood, Victoria 3134, Australia
Penguin Books Ltd
Harmondsworth, Middlesex, England
Viking Penguin, A Division of Penguin Books USA Inc.
375 Hudson Street, New York, New York 10014, USA
Penguin Books Canada Limited
10 Alcorn Avenue, Toronto, Ontario, Canada M4V 3B2
Penguin Books (N.Z.) Ltd
182-190 Wairau Road, Auckland 10, New Zealand

First published by Penguin Books Australia, 1993
Published in Puffin, 1994
10 9 8 7 6 5 4 3 2 1

Typeset in 11/14 pt. Garamond Light by Midland Typesetters, Maryborough, Victoria
Made and printed in Australia by Australian Print Group, Maryborough, Victoria

National Library of Australia
Cataloguing-in-Publication data:

Gleeson, Libby, 1950–
Love me, love me not.
ISBN 0 14 036820 5.
I. Title
A823.3

Acknowledgements
Two of the stories in this book were first published in slightly different forms as follows: 'Fran' – first published as 'Her Room' in *Goodbye and Hello* (eds. Corcoran & Tyrrell, Viking 1992, Puffin 1993); 'Cass' – first published as 'In the Swim' in *Landmarks* (ed. Wheatley, Turton & Chambers 1991, Puffin 1993).

CONTENTS

Acknowledgement
This book was written with the assistance of the Literature Board of the Australia Council.

FRAN

WELCOME TO BAYNTON,
A TIDY TOWN.
POPULATION 6,500.
DRIVE CAREFULLY.

'Population's the same,' said Sam.

The car slowed.

'What did you expect?' Lyn was looking out the other side window. 'We haven't even been gone that long.'

'Nine months, two weeks and three days,' said Fran.

Lyn looked down at her younger sister. 'Why don't you work it out in minutes?'

'I'd need a calculator.' Fran lifted her fringe and wiped her thumb across her forehead and the sweat trickled down the back of her hand. She flicked it at Lyn.

'Quit it. God, you're childish.'

'Shh. We're nearly there.' Their mother shifted in the front seat and glanced over her shoulder. 'Just hold the fights for another ten minutes.'

'I'm hot,' said Sam. He stretched forward, pulling his wet T-shirt from where it had stuck to the seat.

'I don't know why we had to come,' said Lyn. 'Why couldn't we just go straight down to the beach?'

'Marlene asked us to call in for lunch,' their mother said. 'And I wouldn't mind seeing the house again. And my garden. We'll still get to the coast before dark.'

'Who wants to go back to that dump. I don't care if I never see that house again,' said Lyn.

'I do,' said Fran. She saw it all the time. At night Lyn's even breathing was the only sound in their room and, unable to sleep, Fran would walk herself around and around the old house, the yard, the back veranda, down the hallway to her own space. At school when Cass and Maria and Cathy talked on, their voices merging into some kind of background hum until Rebecca hissed at them to be quiet. Anywhere she was alone, Fran felt her way back to that other room. Her room. It had been hers from the beginning. It was in between the dining room and the room where her parents slept. Too close to them for Lyn's liking. She'd moved out to a larger room on the south side of the house when she was ten. But Fran liked the way the wall in her room curved as if to hold her and the sun streamed in, all year round.

She'd painted a picture of it in Art just a few weeks after she'd started at Lewisham High School. She'd sat in the back row of the cold classroom and put on paper the warmth of the rose-pink walls, the billowing curtains, the checked quilt in mauves and red and the handworked rug on the floor.

'Very good,' said Mr Lee and he'd held it up for the whole class. 'You have a wonderful sense of colour and a vivid imagination. I can almost believe it's real.'

'I want to see it again,' she said.

'God, you're a dag.' Lyn elbowed Fran who wrapped her arm across her chest and pulled away.

'Least then I didn't have to share a room with you.'

Their mother turned round, 'Would you two stop it! You've been at each other ever since we started out this morning. Look out the windows. See if you recognise anyone doing their shopping.'

'It's ten o'clock in the morning, Mum. No one gets up that early,' said Lyn.

'No one between the ages of twelve and twenty,' said their father as he swung the car left into the main street.

Sam grinned at his sisters. 'That's us. So who else matters?'

Fran turned her back on Lyn and looked through Sam's window. Robyn might be out, hanging round the corner, waiting for some of the other kids from her class, or the kids from the swimming club. They wouldn't've changed too much. Not in nine months, two weeks and three days.

'Get off,' said Sam. 'I'm hot.'

They passed the pub on the corner, the real-estate agent, the Paragon cafe and Thompson the haberdashers.

'Looks like he hasn't changed anything in the window since we left.' Their mother laughed at the old-fashioned model, standing in corsets and bra, gesturing towards rows of other underwear. She put her hand on their father's knee. He covered it with his own hand for a moment but then took it away to change gear.

Little kids clustered around a street stall out the front of Coles. There were tables selling cakes and toffees, home-made jams and coat-hangers lost in crocheted covers.

'Is that Mrs McIntosh, from the Presbyterian Church?' Their mother pointed and swung round as the car kept moving.

'C'mon, Mum,' said Sam. 'It probably wasn't. You didn't know everyone in town.'

Around the next corner was the Catholic church, the Masonic Hall and the primary school.

'I remember the day you started school there, Lyn,' said their mother. 'I walked you down the hill, pushing Sam in the stroller. You weren't even born, Fran. It hasn't changed.'

Not even born. B.F. Before Fran. Like Cass sometimes when she talked to Maria and Cathy about stuff they'd done in primary school before Fran came. They'd sit on the rough wooden benches under the casuarinas and laugh about Mrs Loveday in kindergarten and how she used to make them dance with Rodney. He had sweaty hands and straggly hair and held the record for burping and farting the loudest in the whole infants school. His hands were dry now and he had spunky bleached hair and Fran knew they all wanted to dance with him again.

They turned from the main street, past a row of houses.

'There's the Dobsons' car out the front of their place,' their mother said. 'I suppose they're still together.' She was speaking to herself, leaning towards the windscreen, looking from house to house. The curtains were all drawn. No one was in the gardens. Their father drove in silence past the swimming pool and the tiny park which was where a house had burnt down and no one had rebuilt it.

'Remember all this, Fran?' said their mother. 'This is the way we walked when we went to the pool.' Hot summer afternoons, five blocks there. Ice-cold spray, long hours in the water and ice-cream under the trees. Five blocks home. The low sun still burning off the bitumen footpath. Home to cool high ceilings, iced water, soothing cream on newly freckled skin. Down the hallway, past Sam's door, Lyn's door, through the dining room, through the glass doors to her room. Fran would lie still on the bottom sheet beneath her posters, her pennants and certificates stuck to the walls.

They stopped talking as they got closer.

Up the hill, past three streets off to the left and the high school on the right. Then suddenly they were at the top of the hill. A thick clump of gum trees marked the school boundary. Houses lined the street opposite. Maccas', Petrovskis', Youngs', Marlene's. Then theirs. What used to be theirs.

The car pulled up just before their old driveway.

'Nearly went in out of habit,' said their father.

Marlene saw them from the front-room window. She waved and disappeared and then came quickly through the front door. She met them halfway down the path and put her arms around their mother's neck and they kissed and hugged each other. Then she kissed their father's cheek. Lyn and Sam stayed back as Marlene moved towards Fran. 'Wow, have you grown! And hasn't your hair gone all lovely and curly.'

Fran hunched her shoulders and looked down at Marlene's feet. The big toe of her left foot was bursting out of the faded red slipper. Fran felt the wet kiss on her temple and smelt perfume, sweat and furniture polish.

'A year of high school gone already. I think you've definitely got yourself another teenager here, Dot,' she laughed.

'Tell me about it,' said their mother and she rolled her eyes towards her other two children.

'I was just getting the place a bit tidy for you. David's out the back. Do you kids want to go and find him?' She put her arm around their mother. 'We've got some catching up to do.'

Fran lingered in the doorway. Then she followed her mother and Marlene through the house. Sam and Lyn went down the side path.

'Have you all settled in yet?'

Fran trailed her fingers along the patterned wallpaper. Sprays of violets, daisies and occasional intense bursts of velvet pansies. There was a white crocheted doily under the telephone.

'It's not too bad,' her mother said. 'The house and yard are smaller and there's a block of of units over the back, but Sydney is so expensive and we didn't want to live too far out in the suburbs. You get used to it.' The two women went into the kitchen. Bits of conversation mixed with sounds of the tap being turned on and cups dropping onto saucers.

Fran, in the darkened hallway, stared through the back screen door.

There were no screen doors on the house in Sydney. No neighbours either where you just climbed over the fence and walked in and got a biscuit and a glass of icy cordial.

'. . . seems okay. Lyn and Sam are happy. Fran? Well. Being thirteen. . .' Laughter. 'She's got a few good mates. Nice kids – the ones I've met.'

The yard hadn't changed. Clothes line in the centre. Three peach trees and an apricot tree in a line from the back step to the side fence. Their fence with their old place. Two palings missing from where they used to climb under when they were too small to go over. A gap worn in the passionfruit vine from where they tore the branches when they were old enough to go over the top. Beyond there was the house. All Fran could see was the wide red roof through the purple jacaranda. She moved towards the fence.

'Lyn. Sam.'

Fran looked to where the branches of the fruit tree closest to the clothes line swayed. She saw a red T-shirt, then an arm and then David's head peering down at them.

'Over here. Come up.'

Lyn shrugged and went and sat on the back step. The others went to stand under the tree.

David was balanced on an upper branch, a bucket wedged between his knees. He was picking the ripe fruit, rolling each piece in his hand, checking for imperfections before placing it in the container. Some he dropped into a pile at the base of the tree.

'Do you want one?' he called. Fran nodded and put her hand out. David chose a peach carefully. She watched him as he stretched one arm high above him, pulling the round yellow fruit from a bunch of leaves. He'd grown. His brown curly hair, bleached by the sun, fell almost to his shoulders. Like Rodney's, only longer. He dropped down from the tree and stood beside them, taller than her, taller even than Sam.

'They taste great,' he said.

She rubbed the warm furry skin with her thumb and bit into the soft flesh. The sweet juice filled her mouth and ran down over her chin and she turned away.

Sam spat out his seed and grinned at David. 'How's it going?' he said and punched David, warmly, in the shoulder.

'Okay. How's yourself?'

'Pretty good.'

'Going to the beach for Christmas, ya lucky mongrels.' David went across to the fence and looked at the fruit trees on the other side. 'D'you want to come over?' he said. 'The bloke told Mum she could have the fruit. Most of it's rotten anyway. He's not going to pick it. He's at work till late.' He climbed up onto the fence and balanced there for a moment. 'God, it's hot.' He took off his T-shirt and dropped it with the bucket over the other side. Sam followed him.

Fran looked back at Lyn. She was lying on the veranda, her face in the shade, her bare legs in the sun. Her eyes were closed. Fran picked a flower from the passionfruit vine and traced the purple line that went down into the creamy trumpet and then out again. She tucked it into her hair and swung herself up onto the fence and balanced for a moment on top of the vine and then she jumped down into what was once her own backyard.

The trees were more twisted and smaller than she remembered. Flies and bees hovered over the peaches that had burst open on the grass. David and Sam were already reaching up, searching for ripe, perfect fruit.

Fran stepped carefully around them and went across the yard. She swung on the centre pole of the clothes line, flicking the socks that dangled above her head. A red, two blue and a green. A torn T-shirt, and swimming costume and towel. Then she was under the jacaranda tree, looking up to the flat boards that were the base of the old tree house. Four wide fence palings nailed across where the tree forked. The rope that had hung there was gone. She'd used it to slide down, the skin on her fingers burning. She could feel it now and as well the relief when she let go and fell rolling onto the grass. She breathed deeply. Hot sun on fresh mown grass. She and Sam used to rake huge piles and jump from the rope.

She knelt in the dry grass and looked across the yard. It hadn't changed. Not much. Just needed water and a mower and the fruit picking up. The vegetable garden needed weeding. Only a pumpkin vine straggled from the central mound.

She turned to the house. Purple wisteria dripped from the curving iron roof over the veranda. On the right was the kitchen window. On the left, the floor-to-ceiling glass of the lounge room. On both were blinds, drawn against the afternoon sun. It was just like any other afternoon, playing in the yard, a year ago. When the sun got too hot she'd run up the back steps, grab a drink from the fridge, collapse in a chair in the lounge room, stretch out on the cool floor in her room. Her room.

She went up the steps and stopped. What if it was locked? What if the new man came home? David said he worked late. But if he changed his mind today? What if someone found her? If Mum and Dad knew? Sam and David were up the trees now, talking. She looked towards the next-door yard. Lyn seemed to be asleep.

Fran opened the back door and stepped into the kitchen.

Mum is at the sink shaking the water from lettuce leaves so crisp that they crackle and squeak in her fingers. Then she's stir-frying vegetables and the steam and the smell hit the back of Fran's throat and she coughs.

The kitchen is cool. Fridge. Stove. The same pale-green walls and lemon-coloured blind. The handle on the tall cupboard next to the door still hangs with one screw missing. A breakfast bowl is in the sink and an open packet of muesli and a crushed beer can are on the bench where the blender used to be. The lid is half off the small bin and something smells mouldy. Fran crosses the hall into the lounge room.

She stands in the doorway and stares at the bare walls. It looks the way it did the day they left. Where her parents' wedding photo used to hang over the mantelpiece, there is only a faint dust mark. A double mattress, covered with a striped sheet, is under the window.

Lyn and Sam lie on the floor playing cards. 'Rack off,' says Sam. 'You don't know how to play this game and don't go whingeing to Mum.' Fran goes.

Out into the darkness of the hallway. She doesn't put the light on. She treads on the bare boards that creak and she feels her way, eyes closed, fingertips touching the soft raised shapes of the wallpaper.

But Sam is not here. Fran opens her eyes. He's out the back with David. They are probably not wondering at all where I am, what I'm doing. Move slowly. Where's the creaking board? It's about four steps along. One. Two. Three. There it is. My steps must be bigger now than they were. 'Silly game,' Mum used to laugh. Counting steps. Eyes closed. Feeling the way.

She is in the dining room. Nine steps across to her door. Seven if you take very big ones. Then two to fall on the bed. Play chasings through the house, or hide-and-seek and always Home is in the bedroom. Dive on the bed. Made it. Call 'Home'. I'm safe.

She reaches the door. It is open. The room ahead is dark,

thick curtains cover the windows. She puts her hand up and switches on the light. A glow from a red bulb fills the room. She steps forward. There are black sheets tumbling from the unmade bed. Posters on the wall. Women. Football. Beer. A racing car in red and white. More football. A team in green and gold. She turns. Above the bed in black and white a naked couple embrace in the shower. Beside the window a girl with no clothes on is riding a bicycle. Fran turns again. Opposite the bed, on the wardrobe doors, on the ceiling there are women in cars, on horseback, in the sea. Standing, kneeling, crouching, lying. Pictures with large suntanned breasts, thighs, dark pubic hair, tight, shiny skin. Between the posters, her pink walls are now red. Fran gasps. She is in the centre of the room. Her hands clutch at her face, tug at her hair, run down over her T-shirt, breasts, belly. The passionfruit flower falls onto the floor and she stamps on it, grinding it into the carpet. She is suddenly cold. She spins round, coughing.

She runs from the room, past the bathroom, down the hall. Her shoes pound the lino in the kitchen. She flings open the back door and and stops. The light hits her like a wall. The sun warms her face, her arms, her bare legs. She breathes deeply. She smells warm grass, ripened fruit and somewhere, someone is cooking a barbecue. The boys, stripped to the waist, sit in the middle of the backyard of David's place, slicing watermelon. They don't even notice as she slips quietly through the hole in the fence, dragging her knees through the black dirt. Passionfruit vine trails in her hair.

They stood on the footpath by the car.

'Goodbye, you lot,' said Marlene and wrapped herself around each of them in turn.

Fran was last.

'You're still the quiet one,' said Marlene. 'I can still see you, toddling around, the perfect baby, and just look at you, all grown up.' She kissed her on top of the head.

Fran looked down and then across at David but he was talking to Sam about a new computer game they had at school.

'Get a move on,' said Dad. 'At this rate we'll never get to the camping ground before dark.' He was just opening his door when a car pulled up behind them.

'Hang on, Frank,' said Marlene. 'I'll introduce you. It's the young bloke from next door. Garry.'

Fran watched as the young man got out of the car and came towards her parents. His grey suit was unbuttoned over a blue and white striped shirt. He took off his sunglasses and held his hand out.

'Garry, this is Frank and Dot,' Marlene smiled. 'You know, the ones I'm always telling you about.'

He shook hands and swung his glasses round as he talked. Sunlight glinted off the signet ring on the little finger of his left hand.

'Did you want to go in and have a look? I don't mind.' He smiled at them all.

Fran looked away. She opened the car door and straightened the seat covers.

'No,' said their mother. 'It's okay.' And then, 'I really only wanted to see the garden.'

'I'm not much of a gardener. It's not as good as when I arrived.' He waved at the straggly lawn. 'They look good, though.' He pointed to the huge hydrangeas that stood on either side of the gate. The flower heads were pale blue, round and open, ready for picking. 'Take some if you want to.'

'We're going camping,' said Fran's mother. 'They wouldn't last. But thanks anyway.'

'Any time.'

The street stall had packed up when they drove back along the main street.

'I'm really glad we came,' said their mother. 'Marlene never changes. And didn't that Garry seem a nice young bloke. He didn't have to offer us the flowers.' She turned to her children in the back seat.

'It was boring,' said Lyn.

'David wants to come to our place in the next holidays,' said Sam.

'Fine. What did you think, Fran?'

But Fran wouldn't look at her mother. She blinked and spat on her hands and rubbed and rubbed at the dirt marks on her knee.

THOMAS

'You are not the only person who has ever had to move school.' Thomas's mother scooped a pile of plates from the table and stood up. 'I moved six times when I was a kid. I'm sick of this, Thomas. We've had this out all holidays. You know why we've moved. We couldn't have stayed. My job here is much better. Your father at least stands a chance of getting something.' She stacked the plates on the sink and came back into the dining room. 'Wash those up before you go to school. And do your hair. I've got to rush.' She picked up her bag and leant across the table. 'C'mon, love. It'll get better. You will make friends, you know. You're not a social incompetent.'

'So why did you come to Sydney?' Five of them were sitting with their desks pushed together. Problem solving, Ms Kelly called it. She'd told Thomas to go with them, Troy, Pete, Rodney and Andrew. They'd read their sheets and then looked over the top of their pieces of paper at him sitting quietly, watching them.

'Mum got a job. Dad was retrenched. He reckons he's got more chance of a job down here.'

'Where'd you come from?'

'Dungog.'

'Where's that?'

'Up the bush.'

'Did you live on a farm?'

'No. In town.' Not a farm but a vacant block next door and over the road and kids everywhere. Always kids. His friends. Stacey's friends. Bikes dropped on the grass and on the veranda. Kids playing, eating, sleeping over, disappearing all day and no one worried. Not like now. A small house with no spare room. Empty. Quiet. Just Mum and Dad and Stace. A yard that's full up with one lemon tree and a clothes line. Street after street of old houses. And then the train that roars all day, all night, into town, out of town.

The others were quiet after that. Maybe he should have said a farm. Could've crapped on about horse riding or burning round paddocks in a four-wheel drive. Trouble was, he'd never ridden anything but a bike, unless you counted a Shetland pony at the Show when he was five. And it had trodden on his new white joggers and he'd bawled till Dad bought him pink fairy floss in sticky cellophane.

Thomas scribbled on his sheet. Maths problems were easy. He could manage problems on paper.

At recess and at lunch time Pete and Troy grabbed their bags and raced each other to the canteen and the oval. Rodney usually disappeared with Carol. Andrew mumbled something about the library. Thomas moved slowly, hoping to just hang around the edges.

'How's it going?' asked Ms Kelly. She sat in front of him with his enrolment papers and other documents on the desk between them.

'All right.'

'It's not easy at first, is it?' She tucked a piece of her short dark hair behind her ear and grinned at him, warmly, and he made himself look up at her and grin, a bit, back. She wore dangly gold earrings and a chunky gold chain on her wrist.

At least she was better than Mrs Davies. On the first morning he and Dad had sat in a room full of other new kids and waited for an hour before the Principal could see them. She'd talked about rules and uniform and expectations. Then they'd stood in the steaming courtyard till a Year Eight kid, it was Andrew, came to show Thomas where to go. Dad had put his arm across Thomas's shoulders, nodded towards the office and whispered, 'Crack her face if she smiled.' Trust Dad. He tried to make a joke out of anything. Thomas had nodded but didn't really feel like joking. Dad didn't have to go into a room of thirty kids who all knew each other already.

'It's not a bad place,' Ms Kelly said. 'Most of them only met last year in Year Seven. We get kids from everywhere.' She looked down at the papers. 'And I see that your results from your last school were excellent. Actually I could tell that from the way you worked in my Maths class on the first day. And I've asked around the other teachers and everyone is pleased with you.'

Thomas blushed a bit then. He felt his neck go warm and then it spread up over his cheeks. Stacey used to laugh at him when that happened. 'Red face, red hair,' she'd chant till Mum would tell her to stop and point out that his hair was actually brown.

He shrugged. 'I've got nothing else to do but homework.'

'Well. That'll probably change. Are you interested in hobbies? Sports? Things like that?' She studied his face, still smiling.

'A bit.' Back home he and Dad had bred budgies. They'd built cages all along one side of the shed and they'd calculated the chances of getting certain colours from different pairs. Every day in Years Six and Seven Thomas had raced home to check if there were eggs, if they had hatched, if the babies were flying. He'd fed and watered and cleaned. And then Dad lost his job.

'When you do get involved, don't let the homework slide. It's me they'll send you to and it's not the side of Year Adviser that I like.' She stood up and closed his folder.

Thomas drifted from the staff room to the veranda and then the bottom playground where most of Year Seven hung around. If he kept moving like this the bell would go and he wouldn't have to sit alone.

When he got home on the first Friday afternoon, Stacey already had her homework spread across the kitchen table.

'You're keen.' He dropped his bag and fell onto the sofa. One spring dug into his back and he shifted his weight rolling sideways till he almost fell off onto the lino.

'There's this kid in my class,' his sister's eyes were wide, 'and she reckons that she always goes to the skating rink on Friday nights. She says all the kids go there. When Mum gets home I'm going to see if I can go too.'

'But you haven't even got any skates.'

'You can hire them.'

'What with?'

'I've got a bit of money.'

'She'll never let you, Stace. And even if she does, Dad'll go off his brain. You know what they're like. It's the big city, baby, and you are only in primary school.'

'You are only in primary school, Stacey. I don't know who is going to be there. I don't know what sort of place it is. For all I know it could be a hang-out for junkies and. . . and types that I don't want you associating with.'

'Mu-um.'

'Don't you *Mu-um* me. There's plenty of time for all this when you're older.' She started unpacking a load of shopping that was in plastic bags all over the kitchen floor.

'You mean I can *Mu-um* you when I'm older.' Stacey giggled.

'You know what I mean.'

Thomas waved to Stacey to join him. He tossed her carrots that she stacked in the vegetable tray in the fridge and then they piled apples, oranges, bananas and passionfruit into the bowl on the sideboard.

Their mother looked at them with a tired grin. 'It's so nice to see that you know where these things go.'

'Don't be sarcastic, Mum.' Thomas bit into an apple. 'You should let her go. It's probably all right. And kids in sixth grade are quite big, you know. You're always telling us how kids today are older than in your day.'

'Don't you start.'

'Seriously.'

'I'm the parent round here, Thomas. I'm the one worried sick if she's late home or gets lost, or worse.'

'Nothing'll happen.'

There was silence for a minute. His mother stacked the last packets of pasta and rice into the cupboard and pushed the plastic bags into a drawer.

'Okay.' She folded her arms and leant back against the stove. 'I'll let her go. On one condition. You take her and bring her home. And you stay there and keep an eye on her the whole time.'

'Me?'

'You.'

'I don't want to go to a bloody skating rink with a pile of little kids.'

'I thought you said they were all quite big kids.'

'Well, they are. . . but . . .'

'Please, Tom. Please.' Stacey tugged his sleeve. 'I'll do whatever you want.'

'I don't want anything.'

'I'll wash up all week.'

Thomas shook his head.

'Two weeks. And I'll make your bed for you. Come on. It's a good deal.'

He paused and looked from his mother to his sister. Grinning. Pleading.

'Okay.' There was nothing to do but homework. That and sitting on the floor of his room thinking. Just thinking. 'But forget about the bed. You stay out of my room and when we get there, you've got to do what I say, okay?'

She saluted him. 'Yes, Sir.'

Their father dropped them a block from the skating rink. They walked slowly past the bank, the boarded-up jeweller's and the cakeshop with windows piled high with yellowing cardboard boxes and cakes with painted-on decorations. At the entrance kids stood around in small groups, skates and roller-blades slung over their shoulders. Big kids. Mostly boys. Stacey moved a bit closer to Thomas.

'I can't see Rachel anywhere.'

'She might be inside.'

'She said she'd wait out here.'

'Are you sure she's coming? She didn't have to go home and ask too, did she?'

'No. At least... I don't think so.'

They waited for a quarter of an hour. Then Thomas said, 'I reckon we just go in. There's no point waiting out here. If she's not there, have a skate and then we can just go home.'

'But we have to wait for Mum.'

'I'll ring her up and tell her to come early.'

Rachel was inside. She came skating towards them as they walked around the floor. 'Where've you been, Stacey?' She grinned at Thomas. 'Are you Stacey's brother?'

'You said you'd be outside.'

'Did I?' She kept looking at him, smiling. She had make-up on, green around the eyes and pink on her cheeks.

'Come on, don't take any notice of him,' said Stacey. 'He had to come. Mum wouldn't let me by myself.' She grabbed Rachel's hand. 'Come and help me get some blades.'

'How come you didn't tell me about him?' Rachel glanced back at Thomas as she went with Stacey towards the office.

He stood there for a few minutes and then went and sat on the hard plastic seats that were around the rink. Most of the rows were empty. Across on the other side, a handful of parents watched young children moving unsteadily in a practice area, while even younger ones ran between the rows or climbed over the backs of chairs. Below him, some of the skaters raced and turned and swirled, or cruised slowly, arms entwined. Close to the railing, others staggered and sometimes fell. Rachel sped past, spun round and waved. Stacey pushed herself, out, into the centre.

They didn't have a skating rink in Dungog. At weekends and after school Thomas rode his bike with Jason and Trevor who lived over the back. Swimming in summer. Football in winter. Mum tried to get him to play tennis all year round. Books from the library. Friday-night videos, sprawled on the floor of Trev's sunroom. Just hanging around. Kids with skates went up and down the footpath or in the carpark behind the RSL club. Not like this.

He watched as a girl with long, blonde hair broke away from a group and raced from one end of the floor to the other. Two of the boys chased her but she was well ahead and had turned and started back before they reached the rails. When she got back, she spun round, grinning, and greeted her pursuers with a bow. One turned and skated slowly to the side. He leant over the rail, puffing, and then looked up and recognised Thomas and waved.

'She beat you then, Pete,' called Thomas.

'Yeah. That's Cathy. She always does. Where's your skates?'

Thomas got up and went towards him. 'I don't have any. Never skated.'

'Should try it, mate. It's easy. Go and hire some. Everyone's here.'

'No way. Just look like a big idiot.'

'Suit yourself.' He skated off to where the group was slowly circling. Thomas stayed at the rail, staring after Pete. He watched him push his way between two of the boys. Troy was one, but the other was a stranger. Cathy had her arm around the waist of a tall, fair-headed boy and different girls formed pairs or threesomes, elbows linked or hands held. The music grew faster. They started to race. Heads down, arms flying. In and out of other skaters. They laughed, called and yelled to each other. Thomas turned away, slowly, and climbed the steps to sit on the benches at the top of the stand. He kept one eye on Stacey's red T-shirt and ignored the smile and wave of her friend Rachel.

'You should've been there, Mum,' said Stacey on the way home. 'It was unreal. There was Rachel and me and her next-door neighbour, Sonya, and after a while we got to play all the games and we went really, really fast and we were haring in and out of all these people, mostly really old kids. . .'

'Like ones my age,' said Thomas. He was in the front, staring out the window.

'. . . and anyway a few of them got a bit uptight at us and told us to clear out, but we didn't care 'cause there's nothing they can do. I mean it's a free country and we can do what we like and the bloke that runs it didn't say anything to us, so there.'

'Was she really a pain?' said her mother.

Thomas shrugged. 'It doesn't matter.'

He watched from the edges all of next week. Cathy, the one who skated faster than Pete, sat up the back in every subject. Sometimes with Rodney who was more often with Carol or his mates, Pete and Troy. They were always mucking around, tripping kids in the aisle, chucking rubbers, chewing up paper and flicking it to the ceiling so it stuck there in tiny wads. Cass who was at the skating rink and her friend Maria who wasn't were in most of his classes. So too was Fran. She hadn't been at the rink either. Rebecca, who might've been there, he couldn't be sure, sat in the front row in Ms Kelly's class and always got everything right. 'She's a maths brain,' said Andrew who got put with Thomas for a research assignment in History. He didn't skate either and said he had other things to do with his time, but he didn't say what.

Friday night, Thomas and his father made pizza. They sliced onions and peppers and salami and talked.

'I suppose Stacey wants to go skating again tonight,' said Thomas.

'It's okay,' said his father. 'Your mother's going to take her. We think it's a bit much for you. Older one gets all the hassles, eh?'

'I don't really mind.' Thomas pushed the pastry into shape. Laughing, calling, swirling group. 'It's a bit boring, but it's okay.'

'No need to worry, mate. Mum and I think you've been pretty good about this whole move. We don't want you carting Stacey round all the time. Anyway, Mum wants to check it out herself.'

Thomas spread the filling over the base. But I want to go. Want to watch, hire skates, push off like Stace does, a bit wobbly, into the middle, laughing, calling, racing.

He opened the oven door and the hot air hit him in the face. He pushed the trays quickly into the oven so that the metal clanged and pieces of grated cheese fell onto the floor.

'We'll have a quiet night at home,' said Dad. 'You can choose the video.'

At the weekend, Thomas sat on the back step, flopped on the sofa in front of the television or lay on his bed. He could get a job, a paper round, deliver junk mail, mow someone's lawn. Lots of the houses had narrow strips of grass for a front yard. You could knock off heaps in one afternoon. Then he could buy a pair of blades and teach himself, up and down the hallway or the strip of cement that ran to the clothes line. When he got good enough he'd just turn up. One Friday night he'd speed into the centre of the rink and race Cathy, race them all, race with them, round and round and round.

Stacey went to Rachel's birthday party on Sunday afternoon. Their father dropped her off and then went on to see some friend he'd known years before who might know something about a job. Thomas watched his mother move from the kitchen through the lounge room, wiping every surface with a wet cloth, piling up books, newspapers and clothes into a heap in the middle of the floor. He picked up the colour magazine from the Saturday *Herald*, flicked through it and dropped it on the coffee-table.

'I've only just wiped that.'

'Sorry.' He didn't move.

'Don't just stand there,' she said. 'Pick it up. Put it away. Do something. Give me a hand.'

'It's always me. Stacey does nothing around this place.'

'Stacey's not here. If you want to go out to a friend's place, that's fine by me.' She dropped a pair of thongs, a sports sock and a page of his English homework into his arms.

'I haven't got any friends.'

'Why don't you invite someone here then?'

'Because I don't like any of them.'

'How do you know till you've tried? People take some getting to know. You've never had to try before.'

'It's all right for you.' His voice was rising. 'You knew the people you were coming down to work with. It's easy for you. And Stacey. It's not fair! I hate this place. Bloody Sydney. I hate, hate, hate it.' He was screaming. The sock fell off the pile to the floor.

'Pick that sock up now, Thomas,' his mother screamed back. 'It isn't easy. It isn't easy for anyone. But not all of us give up. Not all of us are so full of our own bloody selves that we don't think others are having a hard time. Your father...'

'And I'm sick of him too,' Thomas hurled the thongs at the wall. He kicked the coffee-table, screwed the paper into a tight ball, spun round and ran down the hall to his room.

'*Thomas!*'

He slammed the door. Dropped to the floor. Head on his knees. Arms hugging. Shaking. Silent.

Thomas was last into the room for Language. Rebecca and Fran stopped their whispering as he joined them at a listening post. Andrew leant forward to speak and then pulled back as Mr O'Brien coughed and then started the lesson. When he turned to the board, a wad of paper clipped Thomas's ear and fell onto his open book.

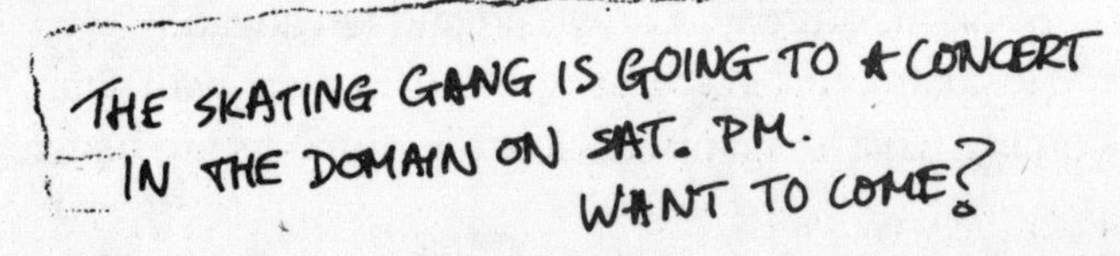

'Who's it from?' He looked to the back of the room and mouthed the words to Pete who shook his head and waved vaguely towards the kids in the corner. Everyone there was turned away from him, concentrating on their earphones. He tucked the note into his pocket. If it wasn't Pete, then who? Andrew had started having lunch with him. He wasn't into anything with the others. It couldn't be him. Rebecca and Katerina talked a lot in Maths extension classes but no one else acted as though he existed.

When the bell went, he hung back, waiting for someone to speak. Cathy was the last to leave. She stood in the doorway, her folder tucked under her arm.

'Well, are you coming?'

Now? Where? The playground? The canteen? Down to the hill around the oval where lots of kids met to eat lunch and watch the sport training?

'Where to?'

'The concert. At the weekend. Everyone's coming.'

'Yeah.' So she'd sent it. Cathy who always had other kids hanging around her. Girls *and* guys. She'd chosen him. He grinned. 'Yeah. Yeah.' He felt the warmth rise up his neck as he walked along beside her, shoulders almost touching. Cathy. He could smell the lemony shampoo from the swinging blonde hair.

'That'd be great.' He couldn't look at her as he spoke.

Fran and Cass were waiting on the path that led to the canteen.

'See you Saturday,' Cathy said and ran ahead.

He heard her voice as she fell in step with Fran. 'He's coming. That's organised. Now the numbers are better.'

He told his mother over the washing up.

'I got asked to go to this concert on Saturday.'

'That's nice.'

'Don't know if I'll go, but.'

'Why on earth not?'

'Well. Would you go if it looked like they just asked you to make up the numbers? I mean someone's probably pulled out.'

His mother was scrubbing the heavy saucepan that his father had used to cook the curry. She rubbed hard at the meat burnt black on the bottom. 'God, it's hard to get this stuff off.'

'Well, would you, Mum?'

She let the pot and the scrubber fall back into the greasy water, and turned to look straight at him. 'Do you want to go?'

'Sort of... Pete says there's going to be all these beaut bands. Jimmy Barnes is playing and Yothu Yindi. I'll never get another chance to see them. Not for free... but...'

'Well, go. It's like the reserve getting a chance to play or the understudy getting on stage for the big night. This could be your lucky break.' She watched him standing there, the tea-towel hanging loose in his hands.

'Trouble is,' he said, 'I've got no decent clothes and it's in a place called the Domain and I haven't got a clue where that is.'

By Saturday, Cathy had conned Andrew into coming as well. He would call for Thomas and then they'd both go to Pete's place where Troy, Cass and Rebecca would be and then they'd meet up with everyone else at the station.

Stacey hung around the front yard. She collected the junk mail, watered the garden, pulled the heads off three dead petunias and tugged out a handful of weeds.

Thomas came out in jeans and a new black and purple mambo T-shirt. 'Wish I had some Reeboks.'

'Mum says we can't afford them. And anyway they'd just get nicked.'

'I'd risk it.' He looked up and down the footpath.

'I don't know why I can't come,' said Stacey.

'You weren't invited.'

'You don't need an invitation to go to a free open-air concert.'

'You do if you are coming with us.' He went back inside then and stood in front of the hallway mirror. He combed his hair for the fourth time and slipped the comb into his back pocket.

Stacey stood in the doorway. 'You should get it cut like Troy,' she said. 'Sort of thick on top and then thinner underneath.'

Thomas pulled at the neck of his T-shirt. He rolled the short sleeves up to his shoulders but there was a line where his pale tan met white skin and he rolled them down again. His mother came through from the back garden and checked that he had enough money, that he knew not to catch a through-train home, that he would look out for drugs, be sensible and have a good time.

'Andrew's here,' yelled Stacey.

Thomas tightened his bum-bag around his hips, pushed his hands deep into his pockets and strolled through the front door.

Pete and Troy, Cass and Rebecca were sitting on the low brick fence in front of the block of flats where Pete lived. He yelled to his mother upstairs and the six of them headed down Centennial Avenue to the station. They spread the width of the footpath, flicking at the shrubs hanging over the fences and the scarlet bottlebrush beside the road. They met Cathy and Fran on the wooden bridge above the railway line. Thomas hung back as they ran down the stairs. He didn't know what sort of ticket to buy or which side of the platform to stand. He moved close to Rebecca and passed her some money when she got to the window and she bought his ticket for him.

Thomas stood for the fifteen minutes in to town. It was the first time he'd been on a suburban train. He hadn't even seen a double-decker train before the move. He looked out at backyards and weed-covered embankments and then the huge brick walls of the factories of the inner city. More and more people got on. He moved into the downstairs carriage and glanced at Cathy as she whispered to Rebecca and Fran, something about Rodney and Carol and how they were supposed to come but had had a fight and backed out at the last minute.

'She's just jealous,' Cass said to Pete. 'Sometimes I think Cathy just organises these things so she can be in the same place as that guy.' She offered around packets of purple chewing gum and then pulled out of her bag a pamphlet about the concert. Six rock bands playing from lunch time till sunset. Speakers and sound systems set up throughout the Domain. Room for close to a hundred thousand people.

'Will there really be that many people there?' said Thomas.

Troy nodded.

'Course there will,' said Cass. 'Were last year. It was unreal.'

They heard the music from the station exit. A heavy, thundering bass. Guitar. Keyboard. Drums. The huge crowd carried them up the steps from underground, across College Street and down Art Gallery Road. Through the lower branches of the giant fig trees they could see thousands and thousands of people, sprawled on the grass, standing, watching, dancing to the music. The crowd started to run. They ran too. They spread out in a long line across the path. Thomas felt his hands grabbed, one by Pete and the other by Cass. She grinned at him. Brown hair flying, cheeks pink, eyes glowing. He hadn't held hands with a girl, with anyone, since folk dancing in sixth grade. He smelt the Harbour salt and felt the wind and the warm sun on his face. Feet pounded around him and over all was the hard, grinding rhythm of the music.

They stopped near a row of tents serving drinks. Thomas stood, hands on hips, trying to catch his breath.

'Unreal, eh?' Cass grinned and shifted from one foot to the other in time to the music.

They bought cold drinks and then pushed their way closer to the front past stalls selling T-shirts, posters, tapes and badges. Cass paid a woman and took five badges, all the face of Jimmy Barnes, and pinned them in a line across her chest.

Cathy danced the way she skated, hair flying, leading the others towards the stage. They followed, Cass, the sweat pouring down her pale neck and Fran moving with small steps, her damp curls stuck to her forehead, her arms still close in to her body.

'How many d'you reckon are here?' Rebecca shouted over the music. She was driving her fists into the air, her black pony tail flicking from side to side.

'Zillions,' Thomas screamed back. He twisted and turned. Wall-to-wall people. More than the whole of Dungog and all in one place. All in one huge paddock. Awesome bands. He was singing along. Slipping into a gap where the stage was in full view. He was dancing. He was grinning. Almost floating. With Rebecca. With Cass, Fran, Cathy. Look at me now, Trev.

They danced and sipped ice-cold drinks and then got up and danced some more. For the last hour and a half, Yothu Yindi was on stage. Song after song, the didgeridoo carried the sound around the Domain, to the tall glass buildings of the city, to the waters of the Harbour. The band sang. The thousands of people sang. And Thomas sang too.

The heat went out of the sun. The shadows of the city buildings began to reach across the grass. The pink and grey sky darkened. The last number was played and then an encore and another and still another. Finally the stage lights went down for the end of a set and didn't come back up again.

'What do we do now?' said Pete. He was sprawled on the grass, shirt off, surrounded by empty cans, bottles and chip packets.

'We can't go home yet.' Cass waved at the people pouring out of the Domain in every direction. 'Let them all go first.'

'Every station's going to be chock-a-block,' said Cathy. 'Let's go down through the Gardens.'

'Where's that?' said Thomas.

Troy rolled his eyes.

'Don't you know anything?' said Rebecca. 'It's kindergarten excursion stuff.'

'Tourist time with country relations.'

'I'll bet you've never been through the Harbour Tunnel.' Troy was pointing at him. 'Or over the Bridge.'

'Yes, I have.'

'Come on, let's take him.' Cathy jumped up and grabbed one of Thomas's hands. Troy grabbed the other one and they yanked him to his feet.

'Hey. Where are we going?'

'You'll see.'

They ran again. This time up and out of the Domain and along the road to the Botanic Gardens. They slowed to a walk then and struck silly poses, pointing and gesturing like tourist guides.

'See this. This is a tree.'

'This is a flower.'

'A bush.'

'A lump of dirt.'

'A hose. It is wet.'

'This is a statue.' Pete leapt up, wrapping his arms around the body of a civic father. 'Ah. Yuk. It's covered in birdshit.'

'You're all mad,' said Thomas. But he spread his arms wide and laughed and ran again with them, follow the leader, to the duck pond and from there to the wall around the Harbour. Ducks, seagulls and other birds took off as they charged along the paths. Couples, walking pressed together, turned away. Cathy leapt up onto the wall, arms outstretched to balance. Pete, then Cass, then Thomas followed. Below them the oil-coloured waters lapped against the yellow sandstone. Ahead was the Opera House, pale and gleaming against the darkening sky.

They jumped down when they reached the gates and linking arms they strode across the forecourt. Men in dinner suits and women in long dresses, young people in jeans, and tourists, cameras clicking, stared as they shuffled to get their feet in time and then in formation danced across to the open-air cafes, the ferry wharves and the station.

'Not yet,' said Cathy. 'It's still too crowded. Let's go round to the Bridge.'

They stopped on the grassy slope by one of the huge southern pylons. Cars, buses and trains roared above them. The wind blew cool off the water.

Cathy pulled them into a tight circle to hear her above the noise. 'I've always wanted to do this,' she said and as the next wave of vehicles thundered above them she spread her arms wide and screamed. The others watched for a moment and then Cass and Pete, Troy and Rebecca began with tentative sounds and then deep, full-throated yells.

Thomas watched. He dropped down on his back on the grass and looked up at the dark underbelly of the Bridge. He spread his arms and legs as wide as possible filling the biggest space that he could. The others dropped to the grass with him. They all held hands, in a circle of cutout dolls. Thomas felt the cool grass, the warm air, the shuddering vibrations and echoing sounds of machines above and friends all around. He opened his mouth and hurled to the world a long, long, wild and joyful cry.

MARIA

He is washing his car. He has taken his shirt off and his back is all pinky-brown with a white line just at the top of his shorts when he bends over. They're red, tight ones like footballers wear. He reaches into the bucket. Sunlight glints off the gold chain around his neck as the white foam bubbles up over his arms and elbows. Bits fly out and get trapped in the curly, black hairs on his upper arm. He leans forward, covering the bonnet with his body. His feet are off the ground, floating.

I can't bear to watch.

Maria had first seen him the day before, coming out of the removalist van. Two huge men in green overalls lifted the wardrobe and the sideboard. Then he'd come down the ramp with a box marked 'speakers' and a lampshade balanced on his head. He was laughing as he ducked beneath the bougainvillea that dripped, blushing pink, over the roof of the veranda. Backwards and forwards all morning, boxes, bulging garbage bags, pot plants. Maria watched until her mother called her to the washing-up and the vacuum cleaner.

Maria stood, one hand holding the edge of the curtain, the other twisting her own neck chain. It was a Christmas present from Yaya. The most expensive jewellery she'd ever had. She rubbed the smooth gold M between her thumb and forefinger, let the curtain drop and turned away from the window. The room was so quiet that she could still hear the splashing of the water on the car, the opening and then slamming of a car door, voices. She lifted the corner of the curtain slightly. There was a woman standing at the front door. She hadn't been there yesterday. She was partly in the shadow and although Maria pulled the curtain as wide as she could and pressed her face against the glass, she couldn't see her completely.

'Coffee's ready, darling.'

'Coming.' He flung the contents of the bucket at the windscreen and headed across the lawn into the house.

After dinner, Maria looked at the Art assignment on her desk. Music came from the television down the hall. She got up and closed the door. She pulled back the curtain and looked out. The car was still parked at the head of the drive where it had been all afternoon. The last rays of the sun fell across it and the small silvery shrubs that lined the path. The front of the house was almost in darkness. She sat down again at her desk and picked up her book. She tried to concentrate on the photograph of a painting of shearers. Arms bent at work. Strong brown arms with curly black hairs, soapsuds and a laughing man with a purple lampshade on his head.

On Monday morning, Maria walked slowly past the house, watching out of the corner of her eye for any movement. The car was gone, the blinds were drawn and the only sign of any change was the stack of empty cardboard boxes and a row of new pot plants on the front veranda.

Cass was waiting at the bus stop. 'D'you do anything at the weekend?'

'Not much. New people moved in next door.'

'Any blokes?'

'No kids.' Brown arms. Black curly hair. 'I didn't go anywhere.'

'D'you watch the movie on Saturday night?'

'No. Mum wouldn't let me. She reckoned there was too much sex and violence.' Laughing with a purple lampshade on his head.

They joked a bit and climbed onto the bus and Cass started to explain just what did happen in the film – who did what and how.

In Maths, Ms Kelly got called to the telephone. 'I know I can trust you to keep working.' She frowned and pointed at the back row. 'Can't I, Troy?'

After a few minutes, Cass nudged Maria.

'Who're you doodling about?'

'No one.' Maria moved her hand to cover the faces with tight black curly hair, sketched in the margin. She hadn't realised she was doing it.

'Come on.' Cass tried to push her hand away. Maria held firm, pressing her short, jagged fingernails into her palm .

'Who is it? Bet it's Ricardo in Year Ten.' She tugged at the book.

Maria tugged back.

At the next table, Thomas put his finger to his lips and nodded slightly towards the door. Ms Kelly had come back and was standing with her arms folded, watching.

Maria bent over her book. The end of her plait brushed the page. 'Bet it isn't.'

On the way home on the bus, Cass kept up her questioning. 'Why won't you tell me?'

'It's no one.' Each denial made her feel stronger.

'I mean, you don't go anywhere that I don't go. I know all the boys you know. I suppose it's just some soapie star or someone in your mind – not real at all.'

Maria just looked ahead.

That afternoon, when Maria turned the corner at the top of the street, she saw the red car parked out the front of the house. Sun gleamed off the chrome and hurt her eyes. She walked more slowly. Would he be there? In the front yard? On the veranda? She kept facing straight ahead but her eyes darted sideways. As she got closer to the car she bent down and adjusted her shoelaces. There was no one to be seen next door. She went slowly through her own gate and up the path.

She kicked her shoes off and cooled her feet on the tiled floor of the TV room at the back of the house. She could see through the branches of the lemon tree, straight into next door's kitchen window. That room was empty. She poured herself a drink and went out onto the back veranda. Nothing moved next door. She could see the tops of the fruit trees, the frangipani and the clothes line. Ginger Cat came out of the patch of long grass and rubbed himself against her leg. She took no notice. He purred and arched his back and the tip of his tail brushed her knee. She dropped into the deckchair and sipped her drink.

Stop thinking about him. Stop. He's old. He's married. She sucked on an ice cube, rolling it round her tongue and then spat it back into the glass. But where is he? Work? What does he do? Where? Why is the car there? Is he in there, asleep? In an armchair? Stretched out on the bed? On his side? On his back, one arm flung across his forehead?

The phone rang. 'I just want to check some homework,' said Cass. 'You know that Maths...' She talked for a few more minutes. Maria waited for the question about the doodling sketches. When it came she didn't answer straight away.

'I don't know why it's such a big secret,' said Cass. 'I always tell you who I think's a real spunk.'

'You do not.'

'What about Chris then, and Rodney?'

'It's no one,' said Maria. 'Just 'cause you never stop thinking about guys.'

'I reckon it's Andrew.'

'Don't be stupid.'

'I saw you looking at him in History on Monday. And he's got black curly hair. And when he had that big argument with Mr Carantinos in Science, you stuck up for him.'

'That's because I agreed with him. He happened to be right, der-brain.'

She hung up soon after that and went back to finish her drink. She sat holding the empty glass in her hand, staring at the fence between the houses. There had been flowers and herbs in the sunny spot there once but no one had kept the watering up to them once summer started and now the mint and the daisies were dry and burnt off. Only the rosemary and thyme had survived.

'Maria? Maria?' Her mother came home from work. 'What on earth are you doing sitting there? The washing's not in.

I don't suppose you've been to the shop for me and you're still in your school clothes. What's up with you?'

After dinner, Maria did her homework with the curtain pulled back and one eye on the house next door. Lights went on and off. Shadows moved against the curtain in the front room. Between Maths exercises and a History quiz, she went out to the TV room. Her father was reading the paper. Maria leant against the window and tried to look as though she was interested in the television guide on the coffee-table. Across the side fence, there was enough light to see that the washing-up was done, dishes were stacked on the sink and two pale-green empty wine glasses were draining on the window sill.

The next afternoon, he was there. He stood watering the plants that ran along the veranda edge and he turned and looked at her as she pushed the gate open. She twisted a long piece of hair around her finger. Her hand trembled.

'Hi,' he called.

She looked at his hand holding the long green hose, at the fine spray that fell on the shiny leaves and the tiny white star-shaped flowers and mumbled 'hello' and ran inside. The front door banged behind her. She stood in the dark hallway, listening to the sounds of her own heartbeat and breathing. The smell of cat and of a damp, closed-up house stirred in her chest and throat. She held her hand to her mouth and ran to the bedroom. She stood at the window, shaking, not daring to lift the curtain. Her legs felt the way they did before an exam, at the dentist or after a long, long race. She fell back on her bed. Her eye caught the image of Mary, framed in gold over her bed, but she looked quickly away and stared at the white ceiling instead.

After a while, she grew calm. He had spoken to her. Her. He had grinned, said 'Hi'. She smiled to herself, then frowned. She'd run from him, not smiled back. He'd think she was an idiot, a dork, a child. She should go right out there now and say 'Hi' and ask him how he was and if he'd settled in and. . . and maybe he would say something more. . . say he'd seen her around and ask her her name and. . .

His name was Martin. Maria's mother learnt that much from the neighbour in the house on the corner when she was at the shop picking up the milk and the cat food. The neighbour, Mrs Parker, wasn't sure where he worked but he left the house early, in a suit, and got home soon after lunch. His wife's name was Jane and her job for a government department in town meant that she was often on the bus late in the afternoon. By the middle of the second week Maria's mother was catching the same bus and they would walk up the hill together and Maria would hear them talking across the geraniums as they each put keys into their front doors. One day Maria surprised her mother by opening the door and helping her with the shopping. She glanced across the yard to where Jane was disappearing inside.

'What a daggy dress she had on,' she said as she unpacked the calamari, the cheeses, oil and olives. 'And her hair is so greasy. You think she'd wash it a bit more often.' Her mother raised her eyebrows but said nothing.

He wasn't always in the yard. On days when there had been some rain he left the garden to itself, but on days when the sun was particularly hot or when warm winds had dried the plants, he was there with the hose as Maria walked along the street. Sometimes, shirt off, he crouched with his hands in the earth, planting tiny seedlings, pulling weeds or spreading rich dark compost. He always smiled and spoke to her. After the third week, she managed to slow down at the gate long enough to look at him and almost smile back.

The first time that he said more than 'Hi', he asked if she'd had a good day at school. She nodded, fumbled the key in the heavy screen door, hurried inside and then lay on her bed till her mother got home. His question played over and over again. She resolved to ask him how work was and she practised it in her head and then went to the bathroom and tried it softly in front of the mirror. She varied the intonation pattern, the tilt of her head and the position of her eyebrows. She unplaited her long dark hair, scooped it up and then let it fall, loose around her face. She undid the top two buttons of her school blouse and let one side drop towards her shoulder. M Maria. M Martin. She was determined to stand calmly by the gate, one hand resting on the letterbox, the other casually in her pocket.

When the opportunity to speak came two days later she pressed her sweaty palms into the fabric of her skirt, opened her mouth and no sound came out. He kept watering the bougainvillea while she, blushing, pushed the key in the lock and almost fell into the hall.

After she had sat in the kitchen, slowly drinking two glasses of cordial and telling herself to calm down, she went through to the TV room. She heard a noise next door and noticed that he had gone out the back and was moving down the path to the back gate. She went outside and stood on the edge of the veranda. She couldn't see where he was or what he was doing. She walked over to the fence and crept along its length, head down so that she couldn't be seen. About a metre before the shed, she knelt and put her eye to the slit between two palings.

He was taking the washing in. At first she saw only his bare legs, mud-spattered from the garden, the muscles taut as he stretched upwards. Then he bent down to pick up a peg and a pair of women's knickers that he'd dropped and she found herself looking him straight in the eye. She froze as still as the paling she was pressed against. He seemed not to notice. He started to whistle some tune that Maria didn't know and gathered up the socks, shorts, bras and shirts and went back up the path inside.

Maria lay on her back in the unmown grass. She tugged the downy head off a dandelion and blew it, chanting softly into the warm air. 'He loves me, he loves me not. He loves me, he loves me not.'

She rolled over onto her belly and pushed herself up. A line full of dry washing challenged her from further down the yard. She ran and started to unpeg the sheets and towels, draping them over her shoulders. Then came her clothes and her mother's, her father's shirts and their large cotton underpants. Everything smelt warm, rich, sun-dried. She ran, overflowing, back into the house.

It was not long after this that her mother came into the bedroom to say goodnight and then didn't leave but sat on the end of the bed and started to talk.

'Is anything bothering you?' she began.

Silence.

'Maria, Dad and I have been thinking that you . . . well, you aren't sort of yourself lately.'

Maria turned away from her, pressing her eyes shut tight.

'You disappear into your room straight after tea. You never talk about school or your friends like you used to. You don't seem to go out with them the way you did a few weeks ago.

How long is it since you went to anyone else's place? And the telephone. You used to sit on the telephone for hours. I like to think that if anything was wrong, you'd come and tell us.'

No answer.

'Have you had a fight with Cass?'

Still no answer.

'You're not having problems at school, are you?'

'No. School's okay.' In a discussion class after recess, Ms Kelly had handed out permission notes for a new programme about AIDS and sexuality.

'Not again,' said Troy. 'I'm sick of doing stuff on AIDS and bloody poofters.'

'That language alone suggests you still need it,' said Ms Kelly. She stood still. Troy had mumbled something about handing round condoms in Year Seven Sex Education and looked down at his desk. 'If it's not on, it's not on,' hissed Pete.

Maybe Ms Kelly thought the boys were juvenile too.

Maria turned over onto her back and her mother put her hand on her daughter's leg.

'There's absolutely nothing wrong, Mum.'

'You're quite sure?'

'Quite sure.'

'Well, just try and be a bit more sociable, if you can.' Her mother moved towards the doorway. 'I'm glad we had this chat,' she said. 'You know, when I was a girl, we'd only been out here a short while and Yaya's head was still in Greece, in the village, with the old ways. I could never talk to her about anything.'

At school, Maria still sat with Cass but she no longer wanted to go with her at lunch time to lie in the sun on the oval watching the teams practising, listening to the talk of what happened at Friday night skating. Cass's plans to go shopping at the mall on Saturday didn't interest her, knowing as she did that what Cass was really trying to do was to meet the gang at the cafe for a drink. All her talk was about Pete and Troy and the new boy Chris who was in Year Nine and had come from Noumea and had a French accent.

Whenever she could, Maria stayed in the library claiming that she hadn't finished her homework or that she had some reading to catch up on. Once Kim was there working and they talked about homework and an English assignment that Kim had nearly finished and that Maria hadn't started. Other times, she sat alone, watching Rodney and Carol and the other couples in the magazine corner, or doodling on the inside covers of her folders, looking at the words on the page but not seeing them.

We are having coffee in a quiet corner of the cafe. 'My wife. . .' he shakes his head. 'You're so much younger but so much more understanding.' Knees touch and our hands. Eyes only for each other.

He is knocking on the front door. He's in a suit. Like out of a glossy magazine. Dark Italian wool, white shirt, gold watch and ring. 'Can I use your phone,' he says. 'Ours is out of order and I need to make an urgent call.'

'Come in,' I say. 'That's fine,' and lead him through the hallway to where the phone is on the kitchen bench. He watches me all the time that he is dialling. Smiling, always smiling, as if he is admiring my hair or the way I arrange myself on the edge of the kitchen stool.

I am in danger. Trapped. Walking home and then suddenly

these men jump out from behind the bushes and they want money and more. They hold a knife at me, rip my shirt. One tries to break the gold chain around my neck. I cannot run. I cannot fight. From nowhere he appears. He is taller, stronger than they are. In one moment he has seen the situation and acted. Wham. Bang. Karate chops and kicks. The men run off. He straightens his tie and dusts off his sleeves.

He puts his arm around my shoulders. 'I'll take care of you,' he says as he leads me home.

It will be midnight. I will be roused by lights and noise next door. I pull on my dressing-gown and rush out into the night. There are police cars, sirens, people everywhere. In the middle of the crowd you are sitting, head in your hands, tears. Someone whispers to us. She's dead. Crashed the car. She had it coming to her. Drink. Speed. I go over to you. 'It will be all right,' I say. 'I'll look after you now.' I wave them all away. 'You can all go now. He's in good hands.'

They fade away, whispering still. 'Such a brave girl. Such a lucky man. Much better off. He'll be all right now. I am tall in my dressing-gown as I lead you inside and we sit on the soft carpet and you rest your head on my lap and I stroke your forehead. 'I love you,' you say. 'Don't ever leave me.'

At the end of the study period Cass pushed her books into her bag and stood up. 'You coming down to the oval for lunch? Pete and Troy are coming, and the others.'

'No,' said Maria. 'I don't feel like it.'

'You never come these days. You haven't really got work

to do. Anyone would think that Kim was your best friend instead of me. You don't really want to go up to the library all the time, do you? I mean. . . are we friends or what?' She turned away and then came back. 'Come on, Maria. I hate going by myself.'

'I don't want to. They're all so babyish. I mean, look at Pete. He struts around, thinks he's so cool. Troy's the same. I'm not the only one who thinks so. You ask Rebecca. She hangs round with them, sometimes, but she agrees with me.'

'How old do you think you are? I'd do it for *you.*'

'Oh. All right.' Maria shrugged, picked up her bag and followed Cass down the steps.

They sat on the mound of grass that looked down to where kids were trying out for pre-season training. Senior boys at one end kicked a soccer ball at their coach in the goal. Girls at the other end ran in formation flicking the red hockey ball across the line. Maria looked up as Pete arrived. He had pulled his long fair hair into a thin ponytail. He sat down in front of her and she couldn't take her eyes off the specks of dandruff dusted over his shoulders. Cass was laughing about something that had happened in Science in first period. Her voice got louder and she leant forward and punched Troy lightly on the shoulder. He slid sideways and flung his arm out to stop himself rolling down the mound. His elbow banged into Maria's hand, pushing the sandwich she was holding hard into her face. Beetroot and tomato smeared over her mouth and cheek and dripped onto the collar of her blouse. Cass, Pete and Troy fell back on the grass laughing.

. . . laughing face beneath a purple lampshade, curly black hair on brown arms. Arms that hold the green hose, red car. Hold her. Hold me. . .

Maria jumped up and ran as fast as she could away from them, slipping and sliding in the long grass, back towards the toilets. She pushed aside the Year Seven girls gathered in the doorway and stood in front of the mirror. She threw scoops of water on her face and it mixed with salty tears to run back over her cheeks and into her mouth.

Maria sat at her window, looking out at the house next door. He wasn't in the yard when she'd come along the street, feet dragging, shoulders down.

M for Maria. M for Martin. I love you. I can't stand boys my own age.

She turned the smooth gold M over in her hands. I want you to have this because I love you. I don't mind if you don't love me, yet.

She smoothed a piece of white tissue paper on her lap and wrapped the gold letter. Take it, please, I want you to have it. It's what I have to give.

'M Martin. M Maria.' She whispered the words, drawing out the sound like a musical note.

She looked through the window again. He must be there. Go up to the door. Knock. When he opens, hand it to him. It's for you. Because I love you. M.

She took a deep breath and stood up.

Her knuckles were white against the green front door. She heard footsteps. It's a gift, because I. . .

The door opened. Jane stood there, curious, and then she smiled broadly. 'Hi. It's Maria, isn't it? Come in. I'm so glad to see someone.'

Maria pressed her hand and its tiny white package deep into the pocket of her skirt. 'I. . . I. . . er. . .'

'I've been sitting here for the last hour, waiting for Martin. I had a flexiday and I had some stuff to do and I'm home early. Would you like something to drink?' Jane walked ahead of Maria into the kitchen. She poured two tall glasses of orange juice and then led the way into the lounge room. Maria sat in a huge green leather armchair. Her feet barely reached the ground and when she wanted to put her drink down she had to wriggle and work her way forward till her arm reached the coffee table. There were vases of flowers, one with bright yellow marigolds, the other a flatter dish with petunias floating against gardenias.

She sat on the edge of the chair.

'Is that the local high-school uniform? It's a really pretty blue. Suits your colouring.'

Maria blushed. She had loosened her hair from its plait and it fell in waves over her shoulders. She couldn't look at the woman.

'You. . . you've got a lot of photos,' she said, finally. She had turned and had noticed black and white photographs, a whole wall of them, framed and hanging behind her.

'It's our hobby. We both love it. We actually met on a course, learning how to do it.' Jane laughed. 'Nothing like bumping up against each other in a darkroom for starting a romance.'

Maria's face burned. She looked away and fiddled with the centre pleat of her skirt, smoothing it down, over and over.

'That was a while ago now. We've been together for years,' Jane paused, 'and now. . .'

Maria looked at her.

Jane was smiling. 'I can't stop myself from telling you. We're going to have a baby. I've just come from the clinic. I've rung Martin and he's on his way home. He was so excited. We've been trying for ages and ages and we were just starting to think that maybe it wasn't going to happen for us.' She winked. 'Mind you, it is fun trying.' She swirled the juice in the bottom of her glass. 'I feel like drinking champagne.' She rested one hand on her flat stomach. 'Hard to believe, isn't it? Inside there is a little bundle of cells starting to grow.' Her hand stayed there, gold and diamond rings flashing themselves at Maria.

She stared, fascinated at the hand on the stomach. The soft skirt fabric, tropical flowers in reds, purples and yellows, fell between Jane's legs. Thighs that parted for him. He entered her body. His child. Their child.

'I have to go,' said Maria. She jumped up suddenly and knocked the coffee-table. The glass fell onto the floor and orange juice seeped into the white carpet. 'I'm sorry. I'm really sorry.' She bent down and wiped at the juice with tissue paper. The gold M fell onto the floor.

'Don't worry,' said Jane. 'That's nothing to what a baby'll do to this carpet.' She picked up the letter. 'What's this? Has it come off your chain?'

Maria nodded. 'It broke at school. I'll have to get it fixed.' She grabbed it and pushed it down into her pocket. 'I have to go. It's great news about the baby.'

Jane leant forward and hugged her. 'You can be our first babysitter.' Her body was soft and smelt cool and fresh. 'Thanks for listening. I have been going on a bit, haven't I? I haven't even asked you what you came in for.'

'Nothing. Nothing really.'

The front gate clicked.

'That'll be Martin,' said Jane. 'Hang on a minute and I'll introduce you two properly.'

'No,' said Maria and pulled back quickly. 'No. You go and meet him. You've got,' she paused, 'to celebrate. I'll let myself out.'

She ran down the back steps and across the yard. She ducked under the fruit trees and around the frangipani. Its heavily scented flowers covered the grass in a cream and lemon carpet. She ran hard over them, gulping and retching, crushing the petals beneath her heavy black school shoes. She reached the point where the fence was lowest. She hauled herself up on the rough wooden palings and balanced there for a moment, looking back down the garden at their house. Soft light came through the vines over the back veranda. She listened and heard nothing. Ginger Cat came stepping lightly along the top of the fence. Maria jumped down and reached out and gathered the cat to her. She knelt, sobbing, on the dry grass, the cat's warm body held tightly to her breast.

CASS

AQUARIUS (JAN 20-FEB 18): Venus, the Zodiac's love star, is moving into your sign this month. This could be the time you have been waiting for. Love may come from someone who has been just a friend before. You're in for a fabulous time if you play your cards right. As your emotions bubble up, move slowly but surely to your goal.

Hot sun. Cass puts the magazine down and spreads yellow zinc on Maria's nose. Maria puts green and pink stripes across Cass's cheeks. They lie face down on their towels.

'What are you wearing tonight?' Maria says.

'Dunno.' Cass watches the water.

Cathy is in there, duckdiving, weaving her way around Rodney, Pete and Troy. She comes up and straightaway is playing with them, laughing, tanned arms shooting spray hard in their faces. Rodney stands with his arms widespread. He's taller than she is with sun-bleached hair, short and spiky on top, longer around his ears. The white foam runs down his face and then he leaps forward, catches her around the shoulders and falls underwater, taking her with him.

'She's so obvious,' says Maria. 'I don't know what he sees in her.'

'Me either,' says Cass.

They roll onto their backs. Cass feels the sweat trickling down her forehead and into her hair.

'Fran said she's wearing jeans and Kim's coming in this sexy new mini-skirt she got for Christmas. What about you?'

'Jeans probably.' Cass isn't thinking about clothes. Eyes closed. Falling underwater with Rodney. His hands pressing on her shoulders. Her hands reaching out, touching him, feeling the short spiky hair, running the length of his body. . .

'I think I'll wear a skirt. That black and gold one with the. . .'

Rolling together to the bottom of the pool then slipping away and bursting out into the air, his hand catching her arm. Tonight, be with me tonight.

'. . . or do you think it'd be better with the green shirt?'

'What?'

'You're not even listening, Cass.'

'I am. I'm just thinking about something.'

'Some*one*, I'll bet. Not the lovely Rodney, by any chance?'

'Don't be stupid.'

'I know you,' says Maria and she glances sideways at Cass. 'He's broken up with Carol, Fran's keen, but looks like Cathy's got her hooks into him.'

Cassie sits up and spreads cream on her pink shoulders. 'She's welcome!'

Cass sat on the edge of her bed. *Love may come from someone who has been just a friend before.* 'Jan?'

'Mmm.' Her sister was at the dressing table, plucking her eyebrows. She watched in the mirror as Cass picked up her tennis racquet from the floor and strummed it like a guitar.

'Have you ever been out with someone who started off being a good friend?'

'Only once,' said Jan. 'It ruined everything. We were mates and now we don't even talk to each other.'

Cass hugged the racquet. She rocked backwards and forwards, her cheek rubbing against the rough towelling handle. A friend since Year Five. Same gang at the pool for two summers. Caught the same school bus home and sometimes ended up standing, shoulders pressed together as more and more kids pushed down the aisle. Mr Sanders made them a pair for tennis at last year's holiday coaching. Rodney said he wanted to go with Carol but Mr Sanders said that was impossible, Cass was much better, and Rodney accepted that and they won the round robin. But he didn't hang around after the match. He went off with Carol straight afterwards.

'But it doesn't have to be like that.'

'Aren't you s'posed to be getting ready?' said Jan.

'In a minute.'

'Mum said you had to come home with Maria's mum.'

'I know. I know.' She turned away from Jan and stared at the faded horse poster above her bed. She is walking home with Rodney. His arm is heavy across her shoulders. His fingers are playing with the gold rings in her ears. His mouth is close to her cheek, her lips.

She rolled off the bed and picked up her jeans and a T-shirt from the floor.

'It's not fair,' she said to Jan. 'You don't have to come home with someone's mother.'

'I did when I was your age.' Jan outlined her lips with a

bright pencil and then filled in the rich colour. 'I didn't get to come home with anyone till I was sixteen. I'm going to get something to eat. What do you want?'

Cass held her breath and pulled up the zipper on her jeans. 'Nothing. I can't sit down in these as it is.' She knelt on the floor in front of the dressing table and sorted through the make-up. Most of it was Jan's. Three different shades of base, two palettes of coloured eye shadows, pencils, blushers and lipsticks. Arranged in bright lacquered boxes. On Cass's side was a tube of pimple cream, a bottle of pale make-up base and an eye shadow container. Blue, green, purple and white. Like the rest of the room. Jan's clothes folded neatly on the chair beneath the travel poster of Paris. Her shoes, in pairs, tucked into the pockets of a hanger on the back of the wardrobe door.

In the mirror, Cass looked at her swimming costume and towel, hanging on the end of her bed, a wet stain spreading over the cotton cover. One of her joggers was on the window sill. She spat on her fingers and slicked her eyebrows down.

Rodney stops and pulls her towards him. His voice so low she can barely hear it. How come we've never done this before? His face comes nearer. Laughing grey-green eyes. Long fair lashes. Warm sweat smell. Aftershave. From the fence behind them jasmine and honeysuckle.

Cass picked up her make-up base and then put it down again. But the jasmine's finished and today he was with Cathy. Tall. Golden tan. Hair almost to her waist. Green eyes flash as she splashes them. The party's at her place. She's organised it all. The last party of summer. She took one of Jan's make-up jars and dabbed the rich sun-tan coloured cream on her face. She worked it in, the way Jan had, from the centre, spreading the mask to her hairline and down to the neck of her T-shirt. Cathy would make sure no one else got near him. Then gold eye shadow, thick on the lids, a brown pencil line along the base of the lashes and smooth black mascara.

'God, Cass.' Jan leant against the doorframe and blew on the steaming coffee. 'That colour's much too dark. You look stupid. Wash it off and start again.'

Cass turned her head and tried to see where the make-up joined her hairline near her ears. 'It's all right. You wear it.'

'It's meant for me. I've got black hair and olive skin. You. . . You've got. . .'

'Say it, why don't you. Mouse brown and lily-white with freckles.'

'Well, that make-up's the same colour as the freckles. Your skin's fair.' She came across the room and reached for the jar. 'It's too dark and it's too greasy for you. Come here. Let me show you how to do it. I'll give you a hand.'

'No thanks.' Cass stood up quickly. The zipper on her jeans caught the flesh of her stomach. She gasped and ducked past Jan and went out to the kitchen.

Cass combed her hair in front of the hall mirror. Her face was now darker than the light brown waves that curled almost to her shoulders. Medium length hair. Medium height. Medium weight. Next to Cathy she was all medium. Sweat glistened on her forehead. A bead of brown make-up trickled down the white skin in the V of her T-shirt. She dabbed at it with a tissue. She took a lipstick from her pocket and applied the red-brown colour. How would his lips feel? Soft and gentle. His hand is in the small of her back. She can feel his muscles beneath the fabric of his shirt. He draws her closer, murmurs in her ear, kisses her cheek, her neck. He holds her for a very long time. . .

'Cass? Come on.' Jan came running down the stairs. 'If I'm dropping you off we have to go now. I'm late already. Jerry'll be waiting. The film starts in twenty minutes. Come on.'

'Truth. Dare. Promise.' Cathy stood on the veranda, framed in the light from the open back door, and clapped her hands. Music was turned off and voices died. 'Come on, you lot,' she said. 'I knew this party was going to get boring. I reckon we should have some fun.' She waved at the three baskets of torn up paper in front of her. 'Who wants to be first?'

Behind her, the house was quiet. Upstairs in a darkened front room, her parents were watching a video. Cass stood up and took a handful of cherries from a bowl. She could just make out the shapes of kids lying on the grass or standing in tight groups around the yard. Most of Year Eight plus some she didn't know from other schools, friends of Cathy's from horse riding and a primary-school ballet class. She stepped back into the shadow of the grapevine. Maria was somewhere near the drinks table. She was talking to Pete and Troy even though she said she couldn't stand them. Thomas was showing off his new silver earring and super-short hair cut. Two years ago these games meant sing a song or dance. But now. . . Cass saw Rodney break away from where he was talking to Fran and Rebecca and move into the centre of the yard. He leant against the clothes line, under the coloured Christmas lights and called to Cathy.

'What've you got for us?' Splashes of red, yellow, blue and green washed over him.

Cass sucked on the last of the cherries and stepped forward.

She could almost reach out and touch him. If only she dared speak. Truth. Make it me. I'll promise.

'You can go first, Rodney,' called Cathy. 'Truth.' She reached into a basket in front of her. 'You'll love this one. What would you most like to do and who would you most like to do it with?' she read.

'Tell us. Go on.' Troy came out of the shadows and dug Rodney in the ribs.

'She's hoping it's her,' whispered Maria. She had come across to where Cassie stood. Pete and Thomas had disappeared.

Cass watched as Rodney grinned, pushed his hands deep into his pockets and shook his head. He looked around. She took a long sip of her cool drink. Me. Let him think me. Kiss. Love. But don't say it. Not out loud.

'No way, Cathy.' Rodney grinned at them all. He didn't mind being first. 'You'd better give me a dare.'

Cathy picked a dare out of the basket. She frowned at it and then read slowly. 'Take the closest member of the opposite sex and disappear down the back with him or her for at least ten minutes.'

Silence. Then giggles. Slow handclapping. Troy wolf-whistled.

Rodney turned slowly around, the same outstretched arms that Cass had seen at the pool. 'I guess that's you, Cass.' He bowed to her and put one hand on her shoulder and made a gesture like a salute towards Cathy.

Cass heard Maria's sharp intake of breath. She saw Fran turn away, frowning. The others were all watching. She walked past Troy, Andrew, Kim, Sandy and two strangers. Across the paved barbecue area. Up two steps through the herbs and a rockery. Then the length of the backyard. She tossed her hair so that it swung against her neck. Crickets drummed. The air was heavy with the scent of frangipani. They stopped behind a straggly oleander. Rodney leant against the fence. They said nothing.

From out of the darkness came Cathy's voice. 'While you two get on with it, we're going to keep playing.'

More whistles.

Get on with it. What? Soft lips. Gentle. Cathy rolling with him, ducking under the water. Muscles beneath the fabric of his shirt. Murmuring in her ear.

Cass dropped the glass. It bounced on her shoe and rolled into the grass. 'Sorry.' She bent to pick it up, feeling the short, dry grass around his feet. She spat out the cherry stone.

'Don't worry about it,' said Rodney. 'Come here.'

She stood up and he leant towards her and put both hands on her sunburnt shoulders. She caught her breath as he pulled her to him. She stood on her toes and strained forward.

Kiss me. Like I've dreamed. Gentle, like Jan says Jerry does. Like in films. Kissing. Mouths open. Tongues. And more. . .

Rodney's lips pressed hard against hers. His mouth was not quite closed and she felt the jagged edge of his teeth. She pushed her lips forward and smelt toothpaste, salami and sweat. She wrapped her arms around him and ran her fingers down the bumps of his spine through the thin shirt. Feelings like shivers ran from her breasts to between her legs to the backs of her thighs. What next? She wanted to swallow. How do you stop? Just pull away? Her toes started to ache. Her forehead was wet and her jeans felt hot and tight. Rodney's hands moved up and into her hair. One knee pushed between her legs, forcing them apart. His lips moved from her mouth to her cheek and then to her ear. That bent her head to one side and her neck hurt. He ran one hand over her shoulder, down her back to her waist. She felt him fumbling with her T-shirt, pulling at where it tucked into her jeans.

'Come on,' he whispered. 'We've only got a couple of minutes.'

He slipped his hand in against her skin and moved it to the catch at the back of her bra. No. Not like this. Cass pressed herself against him. Stopping his hands from reaching her breasts. Out of the corner of her eye, she saw the lights go on in the flats across the back fence. She turned away, burying her face in his chest, rubbing it against his shirt . . .

'Hurry up, you two,' yelled Cathy. 'Food's ready.'

Rodney clutched Cass to him for a moment and then pulled away. 'I'm starving. S'pose we'd better go.' He started to walk back to the centre of the yard. She followed, slowly. This time he didn't touch her.

Cass picked at her supper on the grass with Maria.

'Well,' said the other girl. 'What was he like? Did he ask you to go home with him? You can if you like. I'll fix it with Mum. I'll tell her you've gone with someone else.' She sat, her eyes wide open, waiting for Cass to say something.

Cass sucked on icy watermelon. Pink juice dripped from her chin to the grass. She spat out the black seeds.

'Did he try anything?'

'Just the usual,' said Cass. Was it? Wet kisses. Smell of sweat. Hands running, fumbling.

'Cathy's probably got her claws back in. I just saw them going inside,' said Maria.

Cass knew. She had walked behind Rodney, across the shadowy lawn, to where Pete, his arms around one of Cathy's friends, was cheering on Troy who was dancing, balancing a full glass on his head. He'd kept it up for about a minute and then it had fallen and there were yells and screams as fruit punch, pieces of orange and pineapple ran down his face and inside his shirt. Rodney hadn't spoken to her as Cathy had come up to him and touched him on the cheek.

'Lipstick,' Cathy'd said. 'You ought to clean yourself up.' She'd passed him a drink and as he'd taken it, he'd run his free hand across her bare midriff.

Cass lay, still, in the dark. I guess that's you, Cass. Rodney, sweeping his arms wide, bowing to her, kissing her hard. His hands on her shoulders, in her hair. His mouth on her lips, cheeks, ear. Her own body shivering. His knee pressing. . . Rodney leading back to the party, disappearing with Cathy. . . What else could she have done. . . should she have done. . .?

'You asleep?'

'No.' Cass shielded her eyes from the light and watched as Jan kicked her shoes off and sat down at the dressing-table.

'How was your party?'

'Okay.' She pushed herself up onto her side and watched as Jan spread cream over her face and neck. 'Pretty boring, actually. What about your film?'

'Great.' Jan leant in to the mirror and wiped at the cream with tissues. 'We went to a club afterwards. Did you take all that stuff off?'

'Couldn't be bothered.'

'Mum'll kill you if it gets all over the sheets.'

'It's all right.'

'It'll give you pimples. Come on.'

Cass got up and went through to the bathroom. Mascara smudged under her eyes. The brown make-up was uneven – worn off in places, thick and dark in others. She lathered soap on her cheeks. Jan came and stood in the doorway.

'Any games in the bushes?'

'A bit.'

Jan raised her eyebrow. 'Anyone I know?'

'Rodney, actually.'

'Well done.'

'I didn't choose him. It was a game.'

'Did you win or lose?'

Cass shrugged. 'Dunno.'

'I thought you fancied Rodney.' Jan moved into the room and stretched out a hand so it rested on Cass's shoulder, touching her hair.

Cass shrugged. 'Everyone does.' She filled the sink with water and bent down with her face below the surface. Then she took a towel and rubbed and rubbed her cheeks till they were pink and sore.

Cassie was first at the pool. She lay with a book open in front of her but instead of reading, she picked at the red and green threads in her towel. She kept glancing up to see if any of the others had arrived. Maria came first, waving and yelling from the far side of the grounds. She flopped on the grass beside Cass.

'Heard the gossip?' She unpacked her bag and slowly spread her towel.

'What?'

Maria didn't answer at first. She poured sunscreen onto her palm and wiped it over her face and neck. 'Well, you know how no one could find Cathy and Rodney when we were leaving last night.'

'Yeah.'

'Well, her dad did. In her room. She rang me up and told

me. She wouldn't tell what they were doing or anything but she's not allowed out for the rest of the term. No skating. No pool.' Maria lay down next to Cass. 'Pretty drastic, eh?'

'Must've been something.'

'Shh. Here they come.'

Troy dropped his bag next to Cass. 'Great party last night.'

Rodney sat down facing the water.

Troy gave him a push. 'Lover boy's in a bit of trouble with his mum.'

Rodney knocked him back onto the grass. 'You don't have to tell the whole world.'

'Were you late home?' said Maria. She winked at Cass behind his back.

'And the rest.'

'Shut up,' said Rodney

Troy kept talking. 'First he has this hassle with Cathy's dad and so he's really late home and his mum goes off her brain. Then, when I get round to get him this morning, she's doing the washing. She comes screaming into the room with this shirt that she's just found, the one he was wearing last night, and it was stuffed down the bottom of the washing-machine and it's all covered in this greasy brown make-up. Revolting. Completely wrecked. So then she goes on about how if he must go to parties at least go with girls who don't leave half their face all over his clothes.'

Troy drew his legs up and rolled on his back laughing. 'She left half her face all over you. What did you leave all over her?'

He kept laughing and then Maria joined in.

Rodney looked from one to the other and shrugged and then started to laugh. Behind her sunglasses, Cass blinked and then she too laughed and laughed.

PETE

Pete saw her on the 3.15 train home from soccer. Every Wednesday the Under Fifteens played on the field near Cleveland Street and that meant a bus and a train ride home. Long crinkled black hair above pale skin. Brown school skirt and jumper, sitting next to the aisle, downstairs.

He and Troy were mucking about in the space between carriages. They jumped to touch the ceiling, grabbed the top of the supporting centre pole and then swivelled round, all the way down, their feet flying out to the side. There were other girls all around her in the same brown uniforms, heads together noisily, laughing. She waved her hands as she spoke and shrugged her shoulders. The centre of it all.

Pete stopped. Stared. He couldn't stop looking. Staring. His hands slipped on the pole and there was a rush to his throat and his stomach. He didn't hear what Troy was saying. She looked up and saw him watching her and turned away.

'I said, c'mon mate. It's your turn,' said Troy.

Pete swung half-heartedly. Each time his body revolved he tried to catch her eye. Each time she was looking away, talking, sharing a magazine, head down.

'You're hopeless at this, mate,' said Troy. 'As bad as your soccer.'

''s boring.' Pete leaned against the door opposite the stairs. 'Like a bloody overgrown monkey.' Who is she? Is she younger, Year Seven, or older? She looks about the same.

'What'cha staring at?' Troy fell against Pete.

'Nothing. Get off.' He pushed Troy away and straightened up. Hands in the pockets of his jacket. He flicked his ponytail back. Act cool. Like there's nothing there that really interests you.

Troy noticed the girls at the foot of the stairs. 'What were you staring at *them* for?'

Each time the train stopped, Pete glanced down the stairs to see if the girl had moved. Twice she swung her legs against the armrest to let one of the other girls out of the space between the seats. Once she turned around to talk to someone behind her. The crinkly hair fell almost to the wide belt at her waist.

The train finally pulled in to Pete and Troy's station. Pete hesitated. The doors slowly opened fully.

'C'mon, mate. Let's go and get a drink.' Troy grabbed Pete's bag and leapt onto the platform.

They walked up the hill, gulping from the ice-cold cans, bags slung over their backs.

What stop was she heading for? Is she always on that train?

'D'you wanna come and play some video games?'

Pete shook his head. 'No. I've got some stuff to do at home. See you tomorrow.'

'See you.'

He let himself into the flat and slid his bag across the kitchen floor. He tossed the empty drink can into the bin and opened the fridge. There was a carton of pineapple juice on the inside of the door. He took it out with the bread and cheese, a handful of lettuce, two tomatoes, a cucumber, the margarine, and the salad dressing. Stuck onto the plastic wrap around the bread was a note from his mother and ten dollars.

When you have demolished this loaf, pick up another one at the shops and a kilo of sausages for tea. Ta, Mom.

Pete sat at the sink and slowly ate three thick sandwiches.

Why hadn't he seen her before? He'd been on that train since soccer started, nearly a whole term. She was beautiful. Amazing. Unreal. Not like anyone else. She wouldn't get out of his head. Crinkly black hair. Pale skin. Brown uniform. The 3.15 train. That's all.

Pete lay on his bed and stared at the ceiling. Soccer players stared back. World Cup-winning teams. Italy. Argentina. Posters of players dribbling, shooting, hugging after the goal.

'I don't know what you see in all that soccer rubbish,' his father had said. 'I don't know why you don't want to play football.' He was a Rugby League supporter himself.

'Soccer is real football, Dad,' Pete said. 'Or it is to most of the world.'

'Not round here, it isn't,' said his father. 'They wouldn't know how to tackle to save themselves.'

He tried to do his homework still stretched out on his back. Two pages of Maths problems and an experiment to write up.

Method: Take one schoolboy, thirteen years old, skinny, fair hair. Pretty ordinary soccer player. Put him on a train running west from Central. Add one girl. Name unknown. Address unknown. Age unknown. Everything unknown.

His mother came home from work. 'Are you sick? You didn't get hurt at sport?'

'I'm okay.'

'Well, how come you're out of it, on the bed? Did you pick up the meat for tea? And what's all this stuff left out all over the kitchen? This is not a hotel, you know. You're not a little kid.'

The next Wednesday, she was there again.

Pete had raced from the field the minute the final whistle blew.

'What's the hurry?' Troy had watched him stuffing his shirt into his bag.

'Come on. I want to get the first bus back to the station.'

'What for? Where's the fire?'

Pete had started to walk away. Troy had grabbed his bag and raced after him. 'Okay, okay. But the least you can do is tell me.'

'There's nothing to tell. I just want to make sure I catch the train on time.'

Would she be there? Would she look like last time? Would he feel the same way?

She was. She did. He did.

Pete and Troy, Rodney and Thomas ran up the stairs at Central onto platform 19. It was bare. 3.10 p.m. What if she didn't come before the next train? How could he work it so he stayed on the platform? Pete went across to the chocolate machine. He felt in his pockets for change. Maybe he could go back to the ticket office for some coins. Fall down. Sprain an ankle. Limp to the stairs. Tell the others to go on ahead.

He could hear a train coming. Definitely their line. Voices shouted. 'Come on, Kirsty, Kate. It's our train. Come on.' A crowd of girls in brown uniforms came racing up the stairs onto the platform as the train pulled in.

She was at the back. Pete rushed from the chocolate machine and followed her into the final carriage. Someone pushed him from behind and he bumped her. 'Sorry.'

She didn't reply. She didn't even look round. She ran downstairs with the other girls and this time Pete went downstairs too. He sat a couple of seats behind her. As the train pulled out of the station, Troy came swinging through the aisle. 'Shove over. What're you doing down here?'

'I want to sit down. No law against it, is there?'

He was watching the way a few stray bits of her hair fell down over the back of the seat. A little kid would give them a tug. Just a little tug and then look away, out the window at the graffiti on the brick embankment. She was on the aisle seat again, not talking this time, just looking around while two of her friends never stopped. There was something about the way she held her head to one side.

'I dunno what's up with you. We never sit down here.' Troy's voice was loud.

Pete elbowed him in the ribs. 'Shut up.'

Troy settled back for a moment. 'Ah ha. I see.' He was looking ahead at the girls. 'Now I get you.' He whispered, 'Which one is it?' He didn't wait for an answer. 'Pete's in lo-ve. Pete's in lo-ve.'

'I said shut up,' Pete slid down in his seat. 'I am not.'

One of the other girls stood up and turned and looked at them. As the train pulled in to Redfern she moved out of her seat and walked quickly down the aisle. Her bag whacked Troy's knee as she passed.

'Watch it.' He rubbed the spot and turned to Pete. 'Hope it's not that one. Bitch. That's the leg I shoot goals with.'

'If looks kill,' said Pete, 'you're buried!'

Later, at home, Pete flopped in front of the TV set. He flicked around the channels, kids' shows, quiz shows. He got up and went out to the kitchen, opened the fridge door, closed it again, had a drink of water, dropped his cup into the sink with a clang, kicked the cupboard door shut, took a pen and scrawled his name across the message board by the door. His mother was on the telephone. She covered the receiver with her hand.

'What's got into you? You're as jumpy as anything. Haven't you got some homework to do?'

Pete shrugged. He went down the back stairs and lay on the small patch of grass near the clothes line. This was weird. Not happening to him. Not cool Pete. He'd kissed and danced. He'd even pressed himself against Cathy's friend Mandy when they played the dare game at the last party. It was okay at the time but he hadn't thought much about it since. This was different. He thought about this girl all the time, in his head, in his throat, his chest, his guts... The black and white cat that he'd found behind the chicken shop when he was ten jumped on his stomach and nuzzled his chin. He nuzzled back. 'Cous-Cous, my puss-puss. How are you, girl?' The cat was warm and he stroked and stroked the soft fur till she purred.

Then suddenly he sat up, pushed the cat off his lap, kicked an old soccer ball the length of the yard and ran back up into the flat, into his bedroom and slammed the door.

He left school at lunch time the next day. When the bell went and kids headed for the oval, the library and the computer room, Pete spoke quickly to Thomas and then left.

'Tell Ms Kelly I'm sick. I'm going home.'

'What about the assignments? We have to hand them in today.'

'I haven't finished.'

'You'll cop it.'

Pete went down to the station and hung around in the old waiting room for the train to take him into Central. He didn't want anyone to see him. As the train pulled in he saw Mrs Parker from the house at the end of his street getting off one of the front carriages. She'd happily tell his mother, so he hung back and leapt in the last doorway as the train was pulling out.

There was still an hour to kill at Central Station. He had stuffed his school jumper in his bag so that no one would identify him and now he was cold. He sat on a sandstone block in the weak sunlight and turned out his pockets. A packet of chewing gum, three dollars-fifty, an old note about a Geography excursion, a rubber band and two paperclips. No point going down George Street for a game of pinball. He put everything back in his pockets, bought a packet of peppermint lollies and walked slowly across to the park opposite the station.

Dogs and seagulls hung around the garbage bins. Old men and women sat on the seats or lay on the fallen yellow leaves, in the patches of sun on the grass, beer and sherry bottles beside them. A young couple stood together, bodies pressed against the twisted trunk of a wattle tree. Pete sat down, facing the clock tower. What if she didn't come? What if she was sick, early, late? He watched the huge minute hand edging its way around. He pulled up chunks of grass, and threw them at the birds that came near him. It was stupid. Crazy. She didn't know him. He didn't know her. She probably had a boyfriend. Anyway he was too chicken to speak to her. Even if he had the guts, when and how?

He watched a young woman cross the road and come into the park. She wore baggy pants and a long top in a shiny pink material, trimmed with gold braid. There was gold on her fingers, her ears and around her neck. Her thick black hair fell in waves below her waist. Like the girl he was waiting to see. Hoping to see. He'd never noticed hair before. She kept looking at her watch. Was she waiting too? She sat down between Pete and the wattle tree couple and took out a book to read. After a few minutes she called out in a language Pete didn't understand and waved, and a man who had just come into the park ran towards her. He knelt on the grass beside her and held both her hands and kissed her on the lips. Then he opened the bag he had been carrying and took out a white lace cloth. He spread it between them and placed on it glasses and containers of food. They ate, talking and laughing and touching each other often. Pete lay on the grass and watched. The sun came out from behind a cloud and warmed his face and hands. He could almost taste the sharp, spicy meat, the still warm breads and the sparkling, cool fruit juice.

At three o'clock he slung his bag over his shoulder and dodged the cars and buses on Eddy Avenue. There were already kids racing through the ticket office and up and down stairs to platforms. He stood on the silent platform 19 and waited. The 3.07 came, emptied itself, gathered up a couple of people who looked like they'd been shopping in town and then went on. At 3.14 there was a rush on the stairs and the platform filled with girls in brown uniforms and in maroon and blue. Boys too, in blazers of different colours. All swinging arms and bags and calling with loud shouts over the noise of the train pulling in.

He saw her then and ran from his hiding place behind the chocolate machine, pushing and shoving till he fell into the doorway of the last carriage.

'Watch out,' said some boy, big enough to knock him down with one hit.

'Sorry.' Pete kept pushing his way to the stairs.

The lower deck was crowded so he stood halfway down and watched as she, three rows in front of him, sat talking through four stops. At the fifth stop, two of her friends got out. She stood up to let them pass. As they pushed down the aisle, Pete turned away and read the advertisements above his head.

Safe sex or no sex. If it's not on, it's not on.

When he turned back, she was reading a magazine. The seat beside her was empty. Go and sit next to her. Cool. Confident. Just say excuse me and brush past her. Pete took a step forward. From the other end of the carriage, a woman with a baby in a sling across her front and a young kid clinging to her knee came swaying down the aisle. The kid was crying. The mother grabbed his hand and fell with him into the empty seat. The girl, still reading, slid over to the window.

The next stop was Pete's. He didn't even look out at the platform. Three more stops and she stood up. Pete watched as she lifted her bag above the head of the kid next to her. She pressed her body against the seat in front and edged out in to the aisle. Something about her was vaguely familiar. She turned away from Pete then and went up the stairs at the far end of the carriage. He ducked back out to the doorway. When the train pulled in to the platform, he leant out and watched as she stepped down and headed away from him to the far exit. He jumped down and followed.

People came from every doorway of the train. She was the only one in brown and Pete kept sight of her as he ducked and weaved the length of the platform, up the stairs and across an overhead bridge and down the other side. Men and women in grey suits. She stopped at the shops across the street. She dropped her bag on the footpath and stood looking into a window full of salamis, cheese and tiny jars of pickled vegetables. Pete stood at the newsagents and read the headlines on the paper and magazine banners.

YOUR CHANCE OF LOVE TRY OUR QUIZ

YOUR CAT'S STAR SIGN

The window was full of toys, plastic and china dolls, some smaller than your hand, others as large as a child. Beside them were wooden trucks, plastic trains and construction sets. One was the same as the one Pete had got for his eighth birthday. He and Troy had sat with it for hours after they'd watched three videos and the other kids whose names he didn't remember had gone home. They made a spaceship, a huge, almost spherical object with legs and knobs and antennae. They'd used every single piece and then couldn't bear to take it apart. It had sat on his bookshelf till way past his ninth birthday, maybe even his tenth. Was it in the box under the stairs? Or did it go with other stuff to Auntie Meg's kids?

Pete turned to the delicatessen. The girl with the black crinkly hair had gone.

'So what happened to you yesterday?' They were in the change room before soccer practice. Troy looked up from tying his bootlaces. 'And no bullshit about being sick. I know you didn't go home.'

Pete shrugged. 'I had something I had to do.'

'I don't get it. We're mates, right? But you're just weird lately.'

'I'm okay.'

'You're not in any strife about anything?'

'I said, I'm okay.'

Mr Carlisle yelled at them for an hour. They ran round the oval, they did a circuit of push-ups, sit-ups, stretching, bending and squatting and then sprints half the length of the field. At the end of that, they sprawled breathless on the grass and listened while he talked strategy.

'Strategy,' he shook his fist at them, 'is what wins wars and matches. Strategy beats condition every time. Strategy means use your brains. And when the opposition wakes up to your tactics, you need an alternative strategy.'

Pete watched as a bull ant crawled up a blade of grass. It reached the top and then the grass tilted and rested against Troy's leg. He flicked at it but the ant bit first and Troy swore and Pete laughed. Mr Carlisle frowned.

'This is not a laughing matter, you two. A bit of forward planning and you might just change your life. We might improve on that last game for a start.' He strode around the team, positioning himself in such a way that to look at him, they had to squint and shield their eyes from the sun. 'I never saw such appalling marking. Where was your teamwork? Where the focus? The determination? The plan of action?'

Focus. Determination. Strategy.

Carlisle talked on.

Pete wasn't listening. That's what's needed. A real plan of action. None of this vague following her round stuff. Work out exactly what to do, then do it.

'And next week,' said Mr Carlisle, 'I want to see all of this implemented. No point having a plan like this unless you put it into practice. I'll be watching you.'

Pete sat at the bottom of the back stairs and picked the mud from between the sprigs of his soccer boots. Strategy. That's what was needed. Next time, follow her again. When the others get out at their stop, move up, sit with her, talk to her. He put the boots on the cement path and drew his knees up under his chin. Say 'G'day', or 'Hi. My name's Pete. What's yours?'

He turned sideways and faced the rosemary bush. 'I've seen you on this train before. . .'

'Who are you talking to?' His mother stood above him, holding a half-empty can of cat food and a large spoon. She was frowning and sort of grinning at the same time.

'No one.' Pete stood up and the stick he'd been using fell at his feet. His face was hot and red. He ran up past his mother and went inside and into his room.

Later he stood in front of the mirror in the bathroom. He rubbed at the steamed-up glass and then stepped back.

'G'day. My name's Pete. Do you ride this train often? Hi. My name's Pete. What school do you go to?' He dropped his voice an octave. 'Ciao. I'm Pete. . .'

'Pe-ter.' Loud banging on the door. 'Get a move on, will you? You're not the only person in the family, you know.'

He drew diagrams in the back of his Maths homework book. If strategy one doesn't work, be ready with strategy two. She always sits in the last carriage. Why not get out first, race up over the bridge and then manage to meet her on the other side? Drop something on the stairs just as she's going down. Get in step with her just as she's going over the crossing. Be at the shop just as she reaches the other side of the road. G'day. Great weather we're having.

It rained the next day.

Pete sat in Science and watched the video on reproduction in plants and thought about the girl on the train. Lots of parents fetched kids from the station on wet days.

Hi. I'm Pete. Lousy weather we're having.

It was cold too and he was sniffling. Strategy three, stall for time.

Mr Carantinos flicked the video off and asked Pete the first question. He couldn't answer it and looked to Troy for help. He shrugged and then Cass and Rebecca put their hands up and Carantinos, eyebrows raised and sarcasm in his voice, turned to them. 'So nice to have someone concentrating for a change.'

It poured all weekend. Pete stayed home and watched old videos.

On Monday, the whole of Year Eight were called into the hall. A hundred and fifty kids talking, shuffling feet, laughing and wondering why. Their teachers stood quietly around the walls.

Mrs Davies, her black wavy hair streaked with silver, came down off the stage, close to the front row.

'Today,' she said. 'I want to talk about truanting.' She had the sharp, shrill voice that cut right through you. She cocked her head to one side and waved her hands around as she spoke. 'Now, I know you call it a whole lot of things. It was wagging in my day. Jigging a class. Skiving off. I don't care what you call it. I don't care if it's part of a lesson, a session, half a day or a whole week.'

Pete felt her deep-blue eyes staring at him.

'It's not on.' She looked from him to the kids across the aisle.

Troy dug Pete in the side, 'If it's not on, then it's not on.' They both giggled.

Mr Carantinos stepped in and grabbed them by the shoulders. 'Out,' he hissed and pushed them to stand beside him.

Mrs Davies frowned at them and seemed to address the rest of her comments directly to Pete.

'It's not on because it's illegal. You are not fifteen yet and you are supposed to be here.' She took a deep breath. 'This isn't a major exam year. It's not like Year Ten or Year Twelve. But it is at this stage of your career that you are establishing patterns that are going to determine the sort of final school results that you will earn. Don't waste it. Get your heads down...'

Why was she going on about this? What did she know? Had someone seen him? Someone reported him?'

'Now, I am saying all this because there have been a couple of incidents. Down at the shopping centre and at the station where you, or students of about your age, have been seen in school hours.' Another pause.

Maybe the station master? No. He wouldn't bother. Mrs Parker? And if Mum and Dad knew. . .

'. . . ways of finding out. It is not something that any of you want or need on your school record. I want it to stop and I want it to stop now.'

Pete left the playground again at lunch time. He took his school jumper off and put on a black sweatshirt. He walked along the road beside the railway line to the station one stop closer to the city. It was cold and he walked with his head down kicking the loose stones and tiny clumps of weed along the side of the road. He rode the train past Central, staying on around the City Circle through the dark of the underground sections then bursting into daylight at the edge of the Harbour. He sat for a while in the little park near the ferry wharves, watching the white caps on the waves, hunching his body into the wind.

He hopped back on the trains, changing platforms, staying on the move till it was three o'clock. He arrived at the stairs leading to platform 19 at the same time as a great rush of school students. The clock above the destinations board said 3.12. Pete ran up the stairs, pushing and shoving, being carried along by the rest to the top and then towards the train. He couldn't see her. He tried to see over the kids nearest him but they were too tall. People were already on the train. As the whistle went he leapt forward into the final carriage and the doors closed behind him.

She wasn't there. He ran upstairs through every carriage. In the front one, he stopped. Troy stood on the stairs.

'Surprised to see me? I thought I'd find you here, mate.'

Pete shrugged. 'No law against riding the train.'

'Pretty stupid when you don't have to. When you live a few hundred metres from school.'

Pete didn't answer.

'It's one of those girls, isn't it?'

'Why don't you mind your own business?'

Troy shrugged.

Pete turned his back and then walked slowly the length of the lower level. This wasn't how he planned it. This wasn't part of the strategy. Damn Troy. There were a few girls there in the brown uniform and he wanted to go up to them and ask where she was. But he didn't know her name. What should he say? 'Medium build. Black crinkled hair. Laughs a lot. Waves her hands around when she talks. Beautiful.'

He found her, sitting alone in the last section he reached. She was facing the door where he entered and she looked up from her book and frowned slightly as she saw him come in. He felt silly then and kept walking past her and sat down a few seats further on.

He rehearsed through Redfern, McDonaldtown and Newtown. Hi. G'day. Hello. And then, How come you're on your own?

She read most of the way, head down, paying no attention to the people coming and going from the carriage. A policewoman came and sat next to her at one stop but they didn't speak to each other. When the woman got out, Pete stood up and took a step forward. Go now. Say something. Do it. But what if she wants to be on her own? He was still standing there when the train pulled in at her stop.

Pete took his bag and followed her from the carriage. She didn't turn around but walked quickly to the exit. Again he pushed and darted through the crowds, keeping the brown of her uniform in sight. Over the bridge and down the other side. He forgot Troy. Across the street. She disappeared into the delicatessen. Pete dropped his bag on the footpath and peered in the window. Through the pâtés and pies and cheeses, he watched as she pointed at things and then received them as small white parcels. She grinned at the woman serving her and then they both laughed and Pete found himself grinning too.

When she comes out, I'll speak. I'll tell her my name and that I've been following her and that I think she's just great and can I talk to. . .

She came out. Arms full of shopping. Pete moved in front of her. She stopped, smiled vaguely and stepped around him.

He leapt back to the edge of the footpath, blocking her way.

She stopped again, frowning. 'Yes? What do you want?'

'Um. . .' He looked and saw her eyes were deep blue with long, black lashes.

'Are you following me?' she said.

'Um. Er. Sort of.' He stepped back, stumbled into the gutter and fell on his knees.

She frowned. 'Well you can just quit it, okay?' She turned away from him and pressed the button on the crossing.

He jumped up. 'G'day. My name's Pete.'

'I don't give a stuff what your name is. I don't want to know.'

'I. . . I saw you on the train.'

'How surprising. It's how I get to school.'

'I've been following you.'

'I thought so.'

'And I. . . I really think. . . you're. . .'

'I'm what? What do you really think?'

A horn tooted across the street.

'Kate? Kate? Are you all right?'

That voice. Shrill.

The girl, Kate, turned to him. 'Leave me alone.' One of the

small white parcels slipped from under her arm. 'Get lost. That's my Mum come to get me.'

A thick red salami sausage lay at her feet. Pete picked it up, dusted the dirt off it and held it out to her.

She snatched it from him. 'I'm going and don't you follow me. And don't follow me again, either.'

'But. . .'

Lights changed. The voice again. 'Kate? Is he bothering you? Are you all right?'

Pete looked up. Troy stood on the railway bridge, mouth open. Frozen.

'Kate.'

Pete, hand still outstretched.

Across the street, leaning from her pale green Volvo, Mrs Davies stared at him.

REBECCA

'Canberra? What are you going to Canberra for? Not another netball camp?'

'No. That's next term. Look, there.' Rebecca pointed to the bottom of the note. 'We're going to Parliament, the National Gallery, the National Library. Everywhere that's important. The whole of Year Eight.'

Her mother didn't say anything. She read the form slowly and then turned it over and read the other side. 'I'm not sure.'

'Mu-um.' She drew the word out. Three days and two nights in Canberra. Coach trip down. Motel cabins on the edge of the city. Girls in one block. Boys in the other.

'Come on, Mum. Sign it.' Rebecca folded her arms and tossed her ponytail back. 'Ms Kelly says that everyone should know something of their national capital and of their great cultural institutions.'

'Don't lecture me in that tone. Ms Kelly doesn't have to pay for it. And I don't know who else is going or what the supervision is. I want to think about it for a bit. And talk to your father.'

'Mu-um. It's totally okay. Everyone's going.'

Rebecca's mother pulled her glasses down to the end of her nose and peered over them. 'Everyone's going?' She raised her eyebrows. 'Just the way that everyone in Year Six had roller-blades and everyone in Year Seven was allowed out at parties till midnight? Have you asked every single child in Year Eight?'

'Every single one.' Rebecca grinned and nodded. 'And we are not *children*.'

In the roll class the next day Ms Kelly collected the notes and envelopes with the first instalment of the money. She stopped beside Rebecca's desk. 'Will you be coming?' she said.

'Yes. I just left it all on the kitchen table.'

They looked at maps of Canberra and photographs of the new Parliament House building and the Art Gallery. They divided into groups to discuss each place they would be visiting. They talked about who had been before and when and what they had seen. Maria leant across to Rebecca. 'I'm not allowed to go. Dad never lets me.'

'I'm going,' said Kim. 'My family hasn't been there. They think it's a great chance.'

'Mum says it's a lot of money,' said Rebecca, 'but she's going to try.'

At the end of the morning, Ms Kelly called some of them back. 'Rebecca, Thomas, Kim, Andrew, and Katerina. Have a look at this.' She spread information sheets across her desk.

Mathematics Competition. Where are the mathematicians of the future for the Clever Country? Try your skill at a national competition. Open to all secondary students. Different levels for different age groups.

Thomas looked over Rebecca's shoulder, 'You'd do all right. You're always first.'

She didn't answer.

```
First prize: Computers plus software for the
individual and the school.
```

Ms Kelly pointed to the second column. 'See this stuff about teams and whole-school performance. We've got some of the seniors interested. I thought you lot could represent the younger kids.'

'When is it?'

'Not for a couple of weeks.' She turned the sheet over. 'Four exactly. We can do lots of practice till then.'

'But we've got the excursion.'

'That's only a couple of days,' said Rebecca. She looked at the teacher. 'Does it cost anything?'

'Absolutely nothing.'

'Canberra's freezing at night,' James said over dinner that night. 'When we went for that Geography trip to the snow in Year Ten, we stayed there. God, it was cold. And if you're only in cabins, it'll freeze your bum off.'

'James!' said their mother.

'It's true. I slept in all my clothes with a coat over the top and I was still like ice.'

'Well, in that case, Rebecca can raid your wardrobe as well as mine for things to wear.' She spooned a second helping of creamy vegetable soup into her bowl. 'Thick socks, for example.'

'Sounds like you are going after all,' James said and winked at his sister.

Rebecca mopped the last of her soup with a crust of bread and grinned.

For days there was talk of nothing else but the excursion. They researched Parliament, their local member and current debates. They collected newspapers and art journals and cut out reviews of gallery and library exhibitions. They made lists of essential clothes – socks, long underwear, thick trousers and jewellery and make-up, and they planned seating, dining and sleeping arrangements.

The Maths group stayed with Ms Kelly every lunch time and for two hours after school on Tuesday and Thursday. She had past papers to challenge them and complex exercises from books they'd never heard of.

'It's not just sums, Mum. I can't do it in ten minutes,' said Rebecca. It was almost midnight and her mother stood in the doorway, tapping her watch, talking about how she had an early start in the morning and threatening to unscrew the bulb from the light. The problem was one that Thomas had tried the night before, without success. He'd challenged Rebecca and Kim to solve it before the next class.

'Just give me a bit longer. I've nearly got it.'

Her mother looked at the piles of books on the floor and the screwed-up papers spilling from the basket under the desk. 'I don't know. For someone with an organised mind. . . you can have five more minutes.' She closed the door.

The next day, at lunch, she showed Ms Kelly her working out. 'I just couldn't get the answer,' she said.

Ms Kelly hugged her. 'You are so close. You'd get good

marks for it. Look, everyone. Look what she's done. It's fantastic.'

'Don't ask me how you did it,' said Kim and then Thomas said, 'I was going to bet you couldn't.'

'Money? Ten bucks?'

'Nah. Just a drink or something.'

'Next time.'

With them, and with Andrew and Katerina, she talked problems and solutions, strategies and approaches. Before school. At lunch time and afterwards. In Maths class. In any class.

'What do you talk about all the time?' said Cass. 'You're always with them. You never muck around any more.'

Rebecca couldn't answer. There was order in numbers. You could get answers. 'The competition,' she said.

'You're not even interested in the excursion. You're mad.'

'On the coach to Canberra,' said Cathy, 'you should sit next to Thomas. He really likes you heaps.'

'Thomas?'

'Yeah. He told Rodney. You can sit with whoever you like on the way down.'

Thomas. *Thomas?*

'I know he used to be a bit of a nerd,' said Cathy. 'But he's all right now and you're both brains.' They were sitting on the benches outside the Science labs, waiting for the second bell to go.

'You must be kidding.' Rebecca screwed up her nose. 'I mean he's all right to work with in class. But you just wouldn't think of him like that.'

She never thought of him that way. They sat in Maths, heads

together, shoulders touching, thighs close. She wrote, he suggested, pointed, worked the calculator, both shouted when the answer came. They laughed together. One night he'd rung her, late, just to explain a solution he'd found.

'No, really,' said Cathy.

'When did he say that, anyway? He and Rodney aren't mates.' Rebecca folded her arms. She looked carefully at Cathy. Her eyes were brown with flecks of gold. 'He usually only talks to Andrew. Are you joking or something?' She never normally ate with Cathy, but Maria was away and Cass was practising with the choir and she found herself on the edge of Cathy's group, eating under the casuarinas.

'Rodney told me on the phone last night.' Cathy stood up and tossed her long hair over her shoulder. 'We always talk for hours. I'm going up to the library now to meet him. Why don't you come? Thomas is always up there at lunch time – when you aren't on one of your Maths days, I mean.'

Rebecca looked up at her. Cathy with the green eyes, tanned legs, constant boyfriends. And Rodney. Spunk rat of the year, according to Cass.

'I don't want to see him. I don't believe he said that and anyway, I can't,' she said. 'I have to see Ms Kelly.'

Thomas and Rodney were last into the room after the lunch break. Bags swung over one shoulder. Talking loudly. Rebecca couldn't look at them. As they moved closer to her desk, she knocked her pen onto the floor and then crouched down and felt around the carpet with both hands as if searching. His joggers had slashes of mud and grass stains, so close she could have touched them. He moved on to the back of the room and she slid into her chair.

Had he really said he liked her? Was this like in third grade where people organised boyfriends and then didn't bother to tell them until after the whole thing was over? When Rebecca had to produce the Readers' Theatre at the end of first term, she'd put him in because he was the best in the class at different voices. But you didn't go out with people because they could do funny voices. And she wasn't allowed to go out with anyone, anyway. Just parties and group things. Kissing and touching in the dark. Cathy and Rodney had probably made the whole thing up. For a joke.

Mr O'Brien was late. Rebecca felt someone touch her on the shoulder.

'Are you busy after school?' said Thomas. 'I got some more papers from Ms Kelly. We could do them together.'

Rebecca caught his faint, warm smell and saw the sprinkle of freckles across the back of his right hand. 'I can't,' she whispered, eyes fixed on the book in front of her. 'I have to go to training.'

Netball practice was after school. The session began with a warm-up run around the oval. At the southern bend, near the King Street corner, a group of boys stood, leaning against the fence, talking. Among them, Rodney and Thomas. Rebecca looked away from them. She ran faster, pulling away from the rest of her team. She grabbed the ball back at the court and began the passing practice, throwing the ball hard at Kim, leaping higher, darting more quickly than she could remember doing for a long time. After twenty minutes the coach called a break and they all flopped on the grass of the oval. Rebecca looked casually towards the corner. The boys were gone.

After tea, the phone rang.

'Cathy says that you and Thomas are going together on the excursion,' said Cass.

'Don't be stupid,' Rebecca whispered and held her hand over the receiver as her mother came into the room.

'You mean you're not?'

'Would *you* go with him?'

Cass paused. 'He's all right. He's not ugly or anything. And since he had his hair cut. . . You're always working together anyway. So what's the difference?'

'Plenty. I know he's all right. I don't hate him or anything. I just don't like him that way. You know. Like going together. And anyway, how come everyone's so interested in my love life all of a sudden?'

'Sor-ry,' said Cass. 'There's no need to get so shitty.'

Rebecca lay in the bath after dinner. Warm, soapy water lapped around her shoulders. She ran her fingers over the soft skin of her breasts and belly. She scooped up foam and blew it towards her feet. If it lands on my toes I like him. If it doesn't I don't.

'You're good at problems,' Ms Kelly always said. 'You've got the right mind for them. Logical.'

Treat Thomas, Cathy, Rodney like a problem. Start at the beginning. Cathy says that Rodney says that Thomas says he likes me. Cathy could be lying. Rodney could be lying. Thomas could be lying. Why would they do that? Do I care? Is it all a big joke? But if it's true? Do I say something to him? Wait for Thomas to say something to me? Do I want him to? What will happen in Canberra?

Rebecca sat up and scooped more foam from the surface of the water. She wrote with it on the wall beside her head.

R+T=

She looked at it for a minute and then the foam started to shrink and run down the tiles. She poured shampoo over her hair and massaged it into her scalp.

Does he like me? Do I like him? I told everyone today that I didn't. . . but. . . Shampoo dripped down her forehead and into her eyes. She screwed them tightly. Patterns of the bath tiles made lights in the blackness behind her eyelids. She fell back into the bath, ducking her head under the water. I don't know. I don't know. Warm water washed the shampoo away. Her black hair streamed out around her. She lay with only her nose showing, barely breathing.

'Mum says I have to get some socks from you.' Rebecca stood in her dressing-gown in the doorway of James's room. He was lying on his bed, his hands behind his head, staring at the ceiling.

'Aren't you supposed to be studying?'

'You've gotta take a break some time,' he said. 'Just 'cause *you* can study all night.'

Rebecca sat on the end of the bed. She pulled at the loose blue threads of the cover. She started talking without looking at her brother. 'I don't know if I really want to go on this trip.'

'I thought you were all keen?'

'Sort of.'

'Who's the problem?'

'How'd you guess?'

James rolled his eyes to the ceiling. 'Been there. Done that. I know stuff you wouldn't believe.' He sat up. 'Socks are in the bottom drawer or in the pile of dirty gear next to the door. What's his name?'

Rebecca didn't answer.

'You've gotta know his name. You're not hanging out for some secret admirer, are you?'

'No. Don't be stupid.' Rebecca started pulling pairs of socks out of the drawer. Thick sports socks in football colours. 'These are miles too big.'

'They'll keep you warm in bed. You'll need them. If you're on your own, I mean.' James laughed at her.

She threw a pair of underpants at him that hit him in the face. 'You're no bloody help.' She grabbed two pairs of socks from the pile and left the room.

Year Eight sat in the hall.

'Now remember,' Mrs Davies held up one hand. 'Remember, we expect the very best behaviour. You will have a wonderful time but I do not, I repeat *not* want any reports of anything that will bring disrepute upon this school. You know what I am talking about. I don't need to spell it out.'

'Sex and drugs and rock and roll,' whispered Rodney.

'No, Rodney.' She raised one eyebrow. 'What I mean, in particular, is alcohol.' She grinned a bit then, head to one side. 'And those other things you mentioned as well. There are a lot of you for the teachers to be keeping an eye on – so no fooling around. I don't want anyone getting lost or doing anything that will get them into any trouble whatsoever.' She strode across the front of the hall while she spoke. She was short but she wore very high heels and her loose jacket flapped below her shoulder pads like the wings of a bird about to take off.

Rebecca thought of her starting to soar above them till she was lost in the lights and the rafters of the building. She wanted to laugh but instead slid further down into her seat.

Rodney whispered something to Cathy. Everyone giggled. Rebecca looked around. Thomas was digging Andrew in the side and mouthing something. They both laughed. Ms Kelly and Mr Daley began to check off names.

Rebecca stood with Cass while the bags were loaded onto the coach. They watched Cathy and Rodney pushing to the front and calling loudly that they bagsed the seats at the back. Thomas, Pete and Troy shouted that they were with them. Everyone pressed forward then. Cathy yelled to Rebecca to come up the back but when the crowd had pushed on as far as the middle of the aisle, Rebecca found all the seats further down were taken. She and Cass pushed school hats and shoulder bags into the overhead racks and slipped into a seat beside an open window. They hung out, arms waving at the parents standing around the bus bay.

It took an hour to get out of Sydney. The coach stopped and started in the morning traffic. Red lights flashed. A siren screamed and their driver slowed as ambulances and police cars raced past. Everyone pressed their faces against the glass. Music played over the loud speakers.

'Change the station,' yelled Rodney.

The driver flicked around the dial and when 2MMM came on, there were cheers, claps and cries of 'Leave it there. That's the one.'

Rebecca and Cass pressed their bodies down into their seats and sucked on peppermint Lifesavers and caramel lollies.

At Liverpool, Ms Kelly came up the aisle and sat on the arm of their seat. She grinned and chatted about how mild it was and how it would be colder in Canberra and had they remembered to put their warm socks in their bags.

'You two can be in a room together,' she said and they nodded and she ticked their names off her list. 'And how's Mum feeling about the Maths Competition?'

'Sick of it already,' said Rebecca. 'She reckons I work too late. She reckons if I win anything she's going to flog it to pay the electric light bill.'

One hour out on the freeway, Rebecca stretched and turned around. Thomas was six rows back on the other side of the coach, staring out the window.

'Cass?'

'What?'

'Would you do me a big favour?'

'Maybe.'

'Would you go and tell Thomas to come down here for a bit?'

'I thought you didn't like him.'

'I don't.'

'So why do you want to sit with him?'

'I don't. It's not like that.' Rebecca looked away from Cass. 'I just want to ask him some stuff about the Maths Competition.'

'Not that again.'

Rebecca nodded. Cass stood up.

'How come you want me to ask him? You could just go down there and lean on the seat or get Andrew to swap.'

'Please, Cass.'

'But then I'll have to sit with Andrew.'

'So? He's all right.'

'If you like a little guy who wouldn't know a girl if he fell over one.'

'Don't exaggerate. Come on, Cass. Please.'

'Are you sure you want me to?'

'I'm sure.'

'Really, really sure?

'I am absolutely positive.' Rebecca said it quickly, spitting the words out before they had a chance.

'All right. But you'll owe me for this one.' Cass swayed down the aisle.

Rebecca clenched her fists. Don't say it out loud. Don't let Cathy and Rodney hear. She fell back against the seat as, from the corner of her eye, she saw Cass bend her head and whisper to Thomas. She stared out the window. Sheep and gumtrees. Brown grass. Blue sky starting to cloud over. What if he says no? If he doesn't come and Cass just sways back smirking. Rebecca slid further down as the coach dropped its gears and started a long grind uphill.

Thomas slipped into the seat beside her. 'Cass says you want to see me.'

Rebecca scratched the silver paper around the Lifesavers.

'Do you want one?'

They sucked the lollies in silence.

'The Maths Competition,' she said at last. 'D'you really think we've got a chance?'

'Sure I do. Well. You do. And Katerina's pretty good.'

'But there'll be all these really smart kids from selective schools doing it.'

'Don't worry about them. It's like Ms Kelly says. It's the same as the Olympics. You train hard and you give it your best shot. Anyone can win on the day. At least *you'll* be all right.' He grinned at her as he said that.

'You mean *you* will.' She grinned too. Her shoulders relaxed back into the seat.

He put one foot up against the arm rest of the seat in front of them and folded his arms. 'This is going to be an all right excursion, eh? Freezing, though.'

By the time they were passing Lake George, they had made plans to work all the last weekend on practice papers. They'd speak to the others who were going to do the competition too. Thomas's parents would be fine about them hiding away all day and half the night if necessary. Ms Kelly would just have time to check the work on Monday before the big event on Tuesday.

The coach swung through the gates of the motel complex and pulled up outside.

'I'll see you later,' said Thomas.

Rebecca stood in the doorway of Parliament House. Cold. Wide-eyed. She stepped forward into the space between the pillars and moved from one to the other, holding her palms out flat, letting them slap against the smooth green stone. She craned her neck to take in the ceiling far above her.

'It's magic,' said Ms Kelly beside her.

'Mm.'

Thomas had sat with Andrew at lunch and again on the coach into the city.

Rebecca stood there till Ms Kelly moved on, through the next doorway. She looked for him and then at her work sheet. Questions on the stone and timber used, the physical size of the building, the number and the names of past Prime Ministers. She went across to the stand where leaflets and guidebooks were scattered. Cass came over and sat beside her. Thomas was nowhere in sight.

After about ten minutes, Ms Kelly came back. 'Round everyone up,' she said. 'I want all of you in the Senate for a bit. Come and have a look at politicians working.'

'I'll check if anyone is out the front.' Rebecca dawdled. She stood looking down the long grassy slope to the city below. Maybe Thomas was inside. Or at the cafeteria. Or maybe he'd cleared out. She went back inside and followed the others along the corridors to the Senate chambers.

He was sitting with Andrew and Troy and Mr Daley in the front row, leaning forward, looking over the barrier at the people below. Rebecca sat down next to Cass. 'What are they talking about?'

'Health policy. I think. Something to do with costs.'

'Bor-ing.'

Ms Kelly turned around and lifted her finger to her lips.

Below them, a woman was standing at the table, speaking. From time to time she turned side on and waved a handful of papers in the air. Rebecca stared at the back of Thomas's head. His wavy brown hair was layered in a straight line about halfway down. The thinner bottom section tapered to his collar. He turned and whispered something to Mr Daley and the light caught the silver stud in his ear. At the other end of the row, Rodney and Cathy stood up and made their way quietly towards the back of the chamber. Ms Kelly glared at them. Rebecca watched as Cathy took Rodney's hand and led him out.

Dinner was in the motel cafeteria. Rebecca sat with Cass and Fran. She watched as Cathy, at the next table, laughed and joked with Rodney, Thomas and Andrew. She had on burgundy-coloured ski pants, a white jumper and lots of gold jewellery. It looked so easy. They finished their chicken and chips and three-coloured ice-cream and then Mr Daley spoke.

'You're free this evening. You can do whatever you like.'

Laughter.

'Provided it's within reason. Not too much noise. Remember we aren't the only residents here. Don't leave the grounds, and lights off by about ten o'clock. I'll be wandering round to check.'

'Party's in our room,' Troy whispered to Rebecca as she and Cass left the dining room. 'Don't tell everyone.'

They followed him along the darkened walkway and around past the empty pool to the last room. Noise and laughing from inside. There were kids on the floor, the beds, the chairs and the dressing-table.

Troy passed Rebecca a drink. 'Shove in there next to Cathy. No chairs left.' He squatted back down by the fridge. Cass sat as far from Rodney as she could.

Rebecca took a big sip of her drink. It was ginger ale but it tasted warm and burning in her throat. She coughed. Cathy hit her on the back. 'It's got a bit of brandy in it. Can't you hack it?'

Rebecca didn't reply. She hoped Thomas hadn't heard. He was sitting on the dressing table, half turned away from her, talking to Fran. Maybe he really liked *her* now? Rebecca took a slower mouthful. This time she didn't cough but her mouth curled as she forced herself to swallow. It was like medicine. Troy was telling someone about how he'd brought the brandy from home. Andrew had come in and was going on about some old man at the Parliament who'd complained about the noise that kids were making in the foyer so that he couldn't hear his audio-tour.

Cathy moved away from Rebecca and sat on Rodney's knee. She kissed him hard on the lips for a long time. Rebecca watched his hands move up over Cathy's shoulders and into her hair. Her own body tingled. Rodney and Cathy stood up and slowly stepped over glasses, legs and bodies and left the room. Rebecca could not take her eyes off them.

When the door closed she looked for Thomas. Fran had moved onto the floor and was talking to Andrew. Thomas sat alone. She caught his eye and grinned at him and he came towards her and sat down on the bed. Rebecca took a deep, slow breath.

'I'm feeling stuffy. I'm going for a walk. Do you want to come?' He shrugged. 'Okay.'

It was cold.

Rebecca blew on her fingers and looked sideways at Thomas. His hands were pushed down into the pockets of his jacket. His shoulders were hunched. They walked across a patch of lawn and along the gravel drive to a clump of trees. They talked about the Parliament, the drive back through the city afterwards and the food.

''s cold,' said Thomas. 'D'you want to go back?'

'In a minute,' said Rebecca. They had reached a fence and she climbed up onto the top rail and balanced there. 'It's a fabulous night.' She waved her hand at the stars and the fine wisps of cloud that floated near the moon. 'I could stay out all night.'

'You'd freeze.'

'I'll run to keep warm.' Rebecca leapt down on the other side of the fence and ran away from him in the darkness. He followed, climbing quickly over the railing, chasing her through the long grass, stumbling over the roots of the trees till he caught up with her where the grass sloped down to a creek.

'Warmer now?'

He nodded.

Before he could say anything she placed her hands on his shoulders and reached forward and kissed him on the mouth. His hands held her waist. He kissed her back, but briefly and then he let her go and he turned away and walked upstream.

'Thomas,' she called. 'Thomas.'

He stopped.

No sound but water, trickling over the rocks, falling into unknown spaces. She grew colder.

'I'm sorry,' he said as he walked back towards her. 'I'm sorry.'

Rebecca wrapped her arms around her body and bent her head. Her toes were cold now and her feet.

'I just got a bit of a shock. I never. . .' He shook his head.

'What is it with you,' said Rebecca. 'Are you some kind of sexist or something? D'you think a guy has to make the moves all the time? It's nearly the twenty-first century, you know.'

'It's not that.' Thomas grabbed her by the shoulders. His words came as white breath. 'It's just. I thought. Look. We're friends. Good friends. Mates. I don't think of you like that. I never thought of you like that.'

'Like what?' Rebecca pulled away from him and started to run. Not happily this time. Not playfully, hoping he would follow, but blindly, the cold air hurting her chest. The tears flowing over her cheeks.

The light to her room was still on. Cass opened the door at the first knock and stood shivering in her pyjamas.

'What's the matter? God, are you all right? Where've you been?'

Rebecca pushed past her to the bathroom and started splashing her face with warm water. 'I'm freezing. I've been walking. No, running.'

'Who from?' Cass folded her arms. 'You are so lucky. Mr Daley came round to check if we were all tucked up and I told him you were in the loo and he believed me.'

'Thanks, mate.'

'Was it Thomas?'

'Sort of.'

'What happened? Did you go off together? Does he really, really like you?'

Rebecca shrugged. She dropped her clothes on the bathroom floor and turned the shower on and stood, head bowed, the hot water pelting on her skin, washing the cold away.

Rebecca leaned against the cold grey wall in the National Gallery and looked at the painting opposite. It was huge, gilt framed. The woman in the centre was flinging her body back. Bare breasts. Bare thighs. Large against the bodies of the men behind her, tearing from her the thin fabric of her dress. Fruits and flowers surrounded them.

'Amazing, eh?' said Andrew who had stopped behind her.

She nodded.

He didn't move away but kept looking at the painting while talking to her. 'Are you all right?' he said. 'I thought... I mean... Are you... okay?'

She stumbled away from him. Was it obvious? Had Thomas said something? He shared a room with Andrew. They were mates. Mates.

She was in the rooms of bush crafts. She walked slowly past

cabinets of crocheted and knitted clothes, hand-stitched samplers and cupboards made of kerosene tins. She stopped by pieces of rough-cast furniture. She looked for a long time at a chair made from branches with its seat the slice of timber from the top of a stump. She stretched her hands out and felt the round smooth arms, running her palms along the lengths, letting her fingers feel their way into each tiny knot and crevice. Tears pricked her eyelids.

Fran found her there. She came up and whispered, 'We have to go. Everyone's waiting.'

They walked together, shoulders touching through the rooms and corridors and down the long, long flights of stairs.

When she came into the dining room she ignored everyone, and went across to where Ms Kelly sat. They talked about the Gallery, its architecture, its contents and the bargains that the teacher had found in the gift shop.

'Did you get anything to take home?' she said. Rebecca shook her head. 'Are you feeling all right?' said Ms Kelly. 'You're awfully quiet. Don't go exhausting yourself before the competition.'

Rebecca made herself grin. 'I'm okay. Just a bit tired. I'll go to bed early tonight.' Damn the competition. Damn Thomas.

An hour later she was sitting on the end of her bed, painting her nails and talking to Cass. 'I don't want everyone round here later,' she said. 'You could've asked me first.'

'Ours is a big room,' shrugged Cass. 'It's the last night. Don't be mean.'

'Well, I don't want everyone drinking. If we get sprung. . .'

'It's all gone,' said Cass. 'I should've known you'd be such a goody goody. Are you just worried about Thomas?'

'No. He won't come.'

Fran was first. Her curls, wet from the shower, were plastered around her face. She glanced at Cass and then waved Rebecca to follow her into the tiny bathroom.

'Are you okay?' she said.

Rebecca shrugged.

'What happened last night?' Fran put an arm around Rebecca's shoulders.

'It doesn't matter.'

'Do you want to go round to my room?'

'No. I'll be okay.' Thomas wouldn't come. She would just sit in the half light, quiet, near Fran.

Pete and Troy came in then and others carrying chips and lollies and cold drinks. Cass turned the main light and the bedlamps off and sat down on the floor in a tight circle with Chris and Sandy, Jade and Kim. A soft light came from the bathroom close to the door. They sipped drinks and talked more quietly than the day before. Rebecca sat on the edge of the bed and twisted the cup in her hands.

The door opened and closed and then the bathroom light went out. Cathy and Rodney had entered. They sprawled on the bed near Rebecca, barely visible in the darkness. She heard them whispering, kissing. Her glass was almost empty.

'What happened to Thomas?' said Cathy. 'Where is he?' There was a pause. 'Do you know where he is, Rebecca?'

'I don't know and I don't care.'

The room went quiet.

'I thought you two had something on together.' This time it was Rodney speaking.

'Cut it out,' hissed Fran.

'Well, you thought wrong,' said Rebecca.

'But last night, I heard, it um, ah, looked as if you. . .'

'Looked as if what?' Rebecca held the cup still. Her voice sounded like someone else. Someone a long way away.

In the darkness Rodney bounced his body, humping the pillows, 'Uh, Uh, Uh.' Cathy and Troy were laughing.

'You know what I mean.'

'Don't be stupid,' said Rebecca. Her feet were cold again and her body shivered. Her voice was hard. 'I'm not interested in Thomas.' She dropped the cup. 'Anyone who wants him can have him. I can't stand him. He's a dag. And he can't even kiss properly.'

She stood up. Cathy reached across and flicked on the bedlamp.

Standing, silent, arms folded, in the bathroom doorway, was Thomas.

TROY

'It's chariot-racing time,' the disc jockey in the purple satin shirt, high above the skaters, drawled into the microphone. Strobe lights flashed.

'Come on, Thomas.' Troy punched Thomas's arm. 'You're with me.'

'What do we have to do?'

''s easy. You sit on the skateboard. I push.' Troy reached over the heads of some smaller kids and grabbed a board. 'Come on. Get out of our way.'

'Is it a race?' Thomas tucked his feet up and tried to balance on the narrow board.

'Sort of. No prizes or anything. More just a muck-around.' Troy rested his hands against Thomas's back and started to skate. Slowly at first, past Cass and Fran, Stacey and her friend Rachel. Then they gathered speed down the length of the rink. They bent into the corner. Thomas held on to the wooden platform beneath him. He leant in to the centre, round they went, past the audience of parents on plastic chairs, past Cathy and Rodney, and into the second stretch. Troy took one hand off. He was guiding with only the tips of his fingers. Faster and faster. He picked a gap between couples up ahead. Thomas saw it too. Troy shifted his weight to direct Thomas through. Flash of wheels. Bodies crash.

'Watch it.'

'Bloody hell.'

Thomas and Stacey, Troy and Rachel. Arms. Legs. On top of each other. Under and around each other. Chariots zoom past.

'Watch where you're going!'

'Why don't you skate on the beginners' patch? Dammit, Stace, look what you've done.' Thomas pointed to the long scratch on the inside of the new black roller-blade.

'We've got a right to be here.'

'I'm going to tell Mum on you blokes.'

'What?'

'It's okay, mate.' Thomas stood up and pulled Troy to his feet. 'It's just my stupid sister and her friend.'

'Do you mind?' said Rachel. She stood up, straightened her T-shirt and pushed the loose strands of red hair back into her ponytail. 'You two crashed into us.'

'Yeah,' said Stacey. 'Think you're someone special. Come on, Rache.' She picked up the skateboard. 'Come on.'

Rachel was watching Troy as he settled back onto the chariot. This time Thomas was pushing and Troy rocked, laughing, as they started the run again.

'Troy. Phone for you.'

'Who is it?'

'Some girl,' said his mother, her hand over the mouthpiece.

He took the phone from her. 'Hello.'

Silence.

'Hello?' he said again. 'Hello? Who is this?' He could hear breathing, a faint giggle and then the click of the receiver being put down. He stood there for a moment, looking at the telephone. It rang again and he grabbed it. 'Hello?'

'Hello. Is that Troy?'

'Yeah. Who's that? Did you just ring me?'

'No. No. It wasn't me.' The voice was slow and deliberate and there was something a bit strange about it. Troy couldn't work it out.

'Who is this?'

'Just say it's your secret admirer.'

'My what?'

'You heard.'

'Yeah.' He was shaking his head, frowning. 'But who are you?'

'I think you're really nice. Good looking. . . Um. . . I like your haircut.'

He didn't know what to say then. He stood there in the hallway, hanging onto the receiver till he heard the click at the other end.

'What are you doing?' His brother Jake stood at the back door. 'Has someone died?'

'No. Nothing like that.' Troy put the phone down. 'Just some girl. Says she's a secret admirer.'

'Who do you reckon it is?'

'Dunno.'

It wasn't one of the girls he hung around with. He'd know them, even with a put-on voice.

'It's probably someone really ugly,' said Jake. 'Scared to show her face. Good match for you!'

'Thanks a lot.'

When the bell rang for second period, Troy walked with Pete across to the Science block.

'Guess what I got from Jake,' he said.

Pete didn't bother.

'This,' said Troy and dangled a condom in Pete's face.

Pete grabbed at it but Troy sidestepped and tucked it back into his pocket as they went up the steps.

'What'll you do with it?'

'Have some fun.'

'Don't let Carantinos catch you. He's a mongrel when he goes off his brain.'

'He wouldn't know what it was.'

They laughed all the way to the Science lab.

Mr Carantinos stood at the front of the room, talking in a low voice to a young man dressed in a suit and tie.

'Quiet, you lot,' he said. Folders dropped on the benches, bags slid along the floor and kids called to each other across the room. 'I'm going to be out for a while this morning and Mr Penn is going to supervise. You're to get on with the work sheets from yesterday. No nonsense. I'll expect them finished when I get back. And I'll expect a good report on your behaviour.'

He left.

Kids talked. Rebecca and Katerina looked at the work sheets. Cass looked at Mr Penn and wondered if he was a real teacher or a student. Cathy, in the back row, looked across at Troy. He reached into his pocket and took out the condom. He poked his finger into it and wiggled it at her. She giggled and nudged Rodney.

'Quiet, please.' Mr Penn looked up from his books, took off his glasses and then put them on again.

Troy bent down under the bench and started to blow up the condom. It got rounder and rounder, bigger and bigger.

The tip at the end stood out like a nipple. Cathy stuffed her hand in her mouth. She rocked forward and banged her head. Cass turned round. Troy stuck his chest forward and pressed the condom to it.

'Troy's got a tit, Troy's got a tit,' chanted Pete.

Troy ducked below the bench.

'What's going on?' said Mr Penn. 'You've got work to do.' He stood up and started to walk the length of the room. 'What are you laughing at, girl?'

Cathy coughed and wiped her face with the back of her hand. 'Nothing, sir.'

'Well, get on with it.'

'I haven't got a pen, Mr Penn.' She coughed again.

'Where is it.'

'I don't know.'

Mr Penn took a biro from his pocket and gave it to Cathy.

Behind him, Troy held the opening of the condom to make a narrow slit. Air squeaked out.

'What was that?' said Mr Penn.

'A mouse, sir. I think it was a mouse.' Pete jumped up on the chair.

'Get down, boy. Don't be stupid.'

Another squeak.

'Really, sir. Fair dinkum.'

Rodney flicked a wad of paper at Pete.

Mr Penn looked over his shoulder. He took his glasses off and clutched at them.

More squeaks.

Rodney leaned forward and whispered to Chris what was going on. He passed it on in front of him. Round the class the story went. More voices called out.

'It could be a mouse plague, sir.'

'Truly, sir.'

'We've got them round our house.'

'Get a stick and bash it.'

'They bring the plague, sir.'

'We'll all die, sir.'

'Stop it!' Mr Penn shouted. 'Stop it, all of you.' His hands shook and he scurried to the front of the room and out the door.

Jeers and laughter.

Troy stood up. He waved the condom in the air.

'You are so childish,' said Maria.

'You don't even know what it is,' said Troy.

She blushed.

He went across to the sink and started to fill the condom with water. It quickly overflowed and he held the neck tightly and forced the water down to make a full, huge balloon. He danced across the front of the class, both hands supporting the flopping, rolling ball of water.

Kids were out of their seats, on the benches, grinning, laughing.

'It's missing one thing,' called Rodney from the back. He whispered something to Cathy who took a badge from her shirt. There were noises outside the door. Rodney came towards Troy, the open badge extended. 'Just a little prick,' and he plunged the pointed end into the rubber tip.

The door opened. Water spurted. Straight into the face of Mr Carantinos.

'So. Did you cop it?' They were all sprawled on the grass above the oval. The spring sunshine was warm and they'd taken off their sweatshirts and were using them as pillows. Troy and Rodney flopped down beside Cathy and Pete.

Troy rolled his eyes. 'I am so-o terribly disappointed in you.' It was Mrs Davies' shrill voice. 'This is not a laughing matter.'

Everyone laughed.

'Are they going to send a note home?' said Cass.

'Maybe. It's not like when you got sprung for wagging, Pete. There's no law against condoms.'

'I don't reckon they will.' Rodney's hand rested on Cathy's leg. 'They made Troy turn his pockets out and he had a whole packet there and they took them. You should've seen the look on Davies' face.'

'She had no right,' said Troy. 'They're mine. I might need them.'

'Since when?' said Pete. 'You haven't even got a girlfriend.'

'That's what you think,' said Troy. He lay back on the grass, arms folded behind his head, eyes closed against the sun. 'For all you know, I might have a secet admirer.'

After dinner the phone rang again.

'Is that Troy?'

'Yes.'

'I heard about what happened at school today.' She was breathless. Excited.

'Who told you?'

'Everyone's talking about it.'

'Who are you?'

'I told you. A secret admirer. A friend.'

'Do I know you?'

'I. . . I'm at school.'

'In our year?'

There was a pause. 'I have to go now. I. . .'

'No,' Troy cut her off. 'I don't know anything about you. What you look like.' He wanted to keep hearing her voice. 'What if I make some guesses and you say yes or no?'

'All right.'

'Are you tall?'

'No.'

'Short?'

'No.'

'Medium, then?'

'Sort of.'

'Okay. Have you got blonde hair?'

'No.'

'Black?'

'No.'

'Brown?'

'Sort of again. Mum says it's auburn. I suppose it's reddish brown.'

He didn't know what to ask next. She might hang up at any minute. 'Just tell me what year you're in.'

'I'm in. . . I'm in Year Nine.'

'Year Nine? Which class?'

'I don't want to say any more. I'll talk to you later,' she said and hung up.

Troy sat on the arm of the lounge chair and tried to think of every girl in Year Nine. Not Katie Baillie. She was the best looking one of the lot, a Year Nine version of Cathy, but she was on with Marco in Year Ten. And it wouldn't be Marina or Kylie because they always hung around at skating with older guys from the Catholic college. Pity though. Kylie played lead guitar in the school rock band. Ms Kelly said she had a voice like a young Janis Joplin, whoever she was. Sonya, Lee, Joanna, Michelle. He tried to picture others from that year. None of them seemed right.

The next day, in assembly, he studied the Year Nine girls on the other side of the hall. Rows and rows of girls. Lots whose names he didn't know. Assembly dragged on. Sports results. Uniform lecture. No mention of the events of the previous day. There was a new girl sitting next to Katie. She looked pretty spunky. Might be her. Some hope. She wouldn't know he existed. Anyway, her hair was blonde. Kylie was behind them. She was looking up at the ceiling. Then she turned and looked across to the Year Eight rows. Her eyes met Troy's for a moment and she grinned and then she looked away. Her hair was long, crinkly like Nicole Kidman, and red. Maybe it was her. He'd never spoken to her. He'd only heard her sing at school discos. But she'd looked at him, grinned at him. It must be her.

'Any phone calls?' Troy called to his mother when he came in from school that afternoon.

'No. Should there be?'

'Never know your luck.' He raided the fridge and settled down on the stool by the sink. He sucked the meat off two chicken drumsticks and then ate a bowl of leftover apple crumble.

When he finished, he hung round the kitchen, drumming his fingers on the edge of the sink. He could get a set of drums, practise like mad, challenge for the drummer spot at the next auditions. He paced up and down the hallway, one eye on the telephone. Ring. Dammit ring. He went out and sat on the front step. He pulled new, young leaves off the lavender bush and flicked them towards the gate.

'Hi.' Two girls in the T-shirts of the local primary school, sucking on long red ice blocks, leant over the fence and looked straight at him.

He mumbled, 'Hi,' and looked past them at a yellow Mustang that cruised slowly up the street.

'Don't you remember us?'

He looked back at them. Red ice stains around their mouths. The voice was familiar.

'I'm Rachel. From skating, and this is Stacey. You know, Thomas's sister. We're the ones you bowled over last week.' She stared straight at him with huge eyes.

Why didn't the phone ring? Why didn't these stupid kids buzz off? Primary school kids.

'Yeah. Sure. I remember.' He stood up.

'Where are you going?'

'Homework. I just remembered. I've got some Science homework to do.'

'Something to do with yesterday's lesson?' said Rachel. She grinned at him.

'What do you know about yesterday's lesson?'

'You're famous. Everyone knows about yesterday's lesson.'

'Yeah, well. I'll see you. Okay?'

When the phone rang, later that night, her voice was strangely accented.

'How come you sound different?' said Troy. 'Like you're putting on a weird accent?'

'I don't want you to recognise me.'

'Why not?'

'Then I wouldn't be your secret admirer. You would know me. And maybe you wouldn't like me.'

'I'd like you all right,' said Troy. What other guys in Year Eight had a girlfriend in Year Nine. 'Can I ask you more questions? I want to know a bit more.'

'Okay. But I might not answer.'

'Um. . . what sort of stuff are you into?'

'What do you mean?'

'Sport?'

'Yeah.'

'Music?'

'Yes.'

'Rock?'

'Of course.'

'Playing or listening?'

'That's enough questions. I have to go.'

'I think I saw you in assembly today.'

There was a pause.

'Well, was it you, or not?'

'Maybe.' And then she said, 'I came looking for you, this afternoon, but there were two girls at your gate so I didn't even come down your street.'

'Shit,' said Troy. Red ice-block stains. Yellow Mustang. 'Those bloody kids. They're just a pair of idiots. One of them's the little sister of a mate of mine.'

'They looked interested in you.'

'Nah. They were just walking past. I just happened to be out on the front step.' He thought for a minute. 'Look, this is getting a bit crazy. I think I know who you are. Why don't you meet me somewhere? What about in the library, at lunch time.'

'At school, you mean?'

'Where else?'

'No. No I can't.'

The band had lunchtime practices in the hall. It must be her. 'Well. Where else do you go?'

'I go skating. Friday night.'

'How will I know it's you?'

'You'll know. I have to go now.' She hung up before he could reply.

In Maths on Wednesday morning, Ms Kelly stopped by Troy and Pete's desk. 'I hear you were the star turn in Science on Monday,' she said, one eyebrow arched.

Troy grinned at her.

'Not very amusing,' she said.

'He's going to demonstrate in Sex Education classes,' said Pete. 'Any volunteers?' he called in a loud voice. 'Troy wants volunteers for demos of his special technique. . .'

Loud laughter from the back.

Cass giggled. Rebecca rolled her eyes and kept talking to Fran. Maria made vomit noises and looked away.

They were on the mound above the oval at lunch time. Troy finished his can of drink and burped. 'You guys skating on Friday night?'

'We always skate on Friday night,' said Pete. 'What are you asking for?'

'Just making sure,' said Troy.

'So what's the big attraction?' said Cass. 'Something special going to happen?'

'You're planning to win a race?'

'You've got new blades?'

'You've got some girl?' Rodney spoke last. He rolled over and slapped Troy on the back. 'Come on. Who is it?'

'Poor thing,' said Maria. 'She doesn't know what she's in for.'

Troy grinned and stood up. 'I have to go. There's something I have to do.'

The others clapped and whistled as he went back up towards the main block.

The band was practising in the main hall. A few Year Seven kids hung around in the back rows. You weren't supposed to listen to these practice sessions but if you were quiet, they didn't say anything.

Troy sat down. It must be her.

They were learning a new piece. They stopped, started, talked and argued over the way to do it. Kylie was in the middle. She had on a black T-shirt over her school skirt and black ankle boots. She flicked her long red hair back each time she turned to play again.

Troy slid down in his seat and watched each flick, each sway of her body, each strum of her fingers on the strings of her guitar till the bell rang.

'I saw you again today,' Troy said when she rang just after dinner. He was sitting on the hallway floor, the phone on his lap. He wanted to add something about her playing, tell her how much he liked the song and how much better she was than any of the others. Say something too about how much he looked forward to her ringing. How he waited for it. But he didn't quite have the words.

There was a pause at the other end.

'Are you going skating?' she said, at last.

'You bet. Wouldn't miss it.'

'I'll see you there, then.'

'We could do the chariot ride together,' said Troy.

'Great.'

He pictured her, like in a movie, leaning against the wall, long crinkly hair falling over the hand that holds the telephone. Grinning. Talking to him. When she hung up, he was grinning too and he floated into the lounge room, fell into a chair beside Jake and let his head roll back against the cushion, eyes closed. In the chariot ride he would start slowly, pressing her lightly in the back, feeling her body through the tips of his fingers. Faster and faster they'd go, her hair flying, calling and laughing past the others. Rodney and Cathy, Thomas, Pete, the boys from the Catholic college. Then with one hand, he'd guide her by just the slightest touch, the other hand, waving, raised high above his head.

On Friday he went past the Music room at each change of class. He saw her before the last period of the day. She was in front of him, carrying a guitar case and heading downstairs. He was about to call out to her when two boys from Year Eleven came along the corridor and waved to her. She ran to join them. Troy could hear them laughing all the way to the door out into the playground. She had to be the most popular girl in Year Nine. She'd chosen him. Him. He straightened up and ran his fingers through his hair. Skating. He would see her at skating.

'Still haven't told us who this girl is.' Pete leant back on his chair and looked at Troy.

'You'll see.'

'Tonight? You mean at skating?'

'Yeah. We're chariot racing together.'

'Since when?'

'Since she asked me.' Troy sucked the end of his biro and grinned. 'Well, actually, I asked her, but she said yes. Wait till you see who it is, mate. You're gunna die!'

'Tell us. Go on.'

But Troy just shook his head and kept grinning.

Troy was early. He hung around in the foyer of the skating

rink, blades slung over his shoulder, one hand in the pocket of his jeans. He caught his reflection in the mirror that hung over the racks of chocolate bars, lollies and the ice-cream freezer. Black T-shirt with the short sleeves rolled back twice, faded jeans, torn slightly at the right knee, Reeboks. Hair spiked up. Maybe he should get an earring. When he suggested it at the dinner table, once, Dad said, 'Who do you think you are, a pirate?'

Pete was the next to arrive. 'Well, mate. Where is she?'

'No worries. She'll be here.'

They went through to the main rink and found a spot on the benches to leave their gear.

'Bet you're just making all this up,' said Pete.

'She's real all right.' said Troy. He didn't wait for Pete but skated out into the centre of the floor. He wanted to be out there when she arrived, haring around, stopping, turning. In the centre of it all.

Rodney and Cathy arrived, then Thomas and his sister. Her friend was with them and she stopped at the rail and hung over it, like she was looking for someone. Then she came onto the floor and raced around, leaping and turning as if this was a performance and something important depended on it.

Kylie arrived. She was with her friend Marina and at first they sat up on the seats, watching the skaters on the floor and talking and occasionally pointing at them. Thomas skated around with Troy.

'Hear you're getting on with someone tonight,' he said.

'You heard right,' said Troy.

There was a speed-skating race, a game of wall-to-wall and a free skating segment. Troy tried to get closer to Kylie but each time she was hemmed in by Marina or by crowds of kids he didn't know. A few times he found himself skating next to Rachel and Stacey and twice they bumped into him and said 'sorry' and giggled as he frowned and turned away.

At 9.30 the voice announced, 'It's chariot-racing time. Choose your partners, please.' They were all sitting out, having a drink. Thomas looked at Troy but he shook his head and grinned at Pete and at Rodney.

'Okay, you blokes,' he said. 'This is the one she promised me.' He stood up and went down the steps to the floor. Kylie was on her own, walking back from the far side. They met at the gate, under the huge strobe light. She stepped around him.

'Kylie?'

'Yes?'

'It's me. Troy.'

'So?' She flicked her long red hair back.

'You know, it's chariot-racing time,' and he swept one hand towards the floor in invitation to her.

'What in the hell are you going on about?'

'You know...' He moved towards her.

'Know what?'

'On the phone... Y... You. My secret admirer. You said so.'

She started to laugh then. Giggles pushed from lips pressed together. Her mouth opened, her shoulders heaved. She laughed louder and louder. Her curls fell over her face. People around them stared. She covered her mouth with her hands and rocked forward. Above them, Pete, Rodney, Cathy, Thomas leaned forward, watching, straining to catch each word.

Troy stepped back. She was still laughing, one hand pointing directly at him. His hand gripped the railing. He stumbled and almost fell.

'Troy. Troy.' It was the voice from the phone. The same voice, calling him. 'Troy. It's me.'

He turned. Coming towards him, a chariot skateboard cradled in her arms, was Rachel.

ANDREW

'Do you think I'm ugly?'

Andrew stood in the doorway of his sister's bedroom. She had a Maths textbook in front of her and was tracing with one finger the pattern of a graph.

'Anna?'

'Mm.'

'I asked you a question. Do you think I'm ugly?'

'No more than usual.'

'No. I mean seriously.'

She turned her chair around slowly. He wouldn't look at her but stared at a pile of clothes on the floor. Her school shirt, socks that were brown at the heel, knickers and a flesh-coloured bra.

'You really mean that as a serious question?'

'Sort of. Yes, I do.'

'Well. You aren't exactly Mr Universe. . .' She leant back in her chair and ran her eyes over his face and body. He blushed.

'. . . but no. You've got two eyes, two ears, no more pimples than the average, the odd muscle. You're not *ugly*. What do you want to know for?'

Andrew came into the room and sat on the end of the bed. He pushed a pile of Ancient History books and notes onto the floor. 'It's bloody Troy. He gets this invitation to Fran's party, right. It's the first one she's ever had. They had this house near Pete's but now they've moved to a bigger place. He sounds off about it all lunch time in front of those of us guys that he knows aren't going. It's him and Pete and Rodney of course and a few others who are in the teams with them. I think the rest are in Year Nine. It's always them. It just gives me the shits.'

'Why don't you and your mates just go? Crash it.'

'And get punched out? You've got to be joking.' He paused. 'What mates, anyway?'

'Thomas. You're mates with him.'

'S'pose so. But even he's going. He's just the big hero ever since that special thing they got in the Maths Competition.'

'You were in that too.'

'Yeah. But I didn't win the prize like they did, did I?'

Anna sat for a minute without speaking. She bunched her knees up and put her arms around them and rested her chin on her hands. She was four years older than Andrew and had a boyfriend, not her first, and she had even been allowed to go away with him for the weekend.

'Maybe you have to get to know the girls a bit better. Sit with them in class.'

'I do a bit. Rebecca and Katerina in Maths. Sometimes.'

'Do you talk to them?'

'Just work stuff.'

'Not that. I mean really talk.'

'But what would I say?'

'Whatever you like. The weather. Your homework. Music. TV. Tell them a joke. Tell them about your collections. Talk fossils. Whatever comes into your head. They won't eat you. It's not easy for them either, you know.'

'Says you.'

'Oh, come on, Andrew. I've been there. Remember? I wasn't always in Year Eleven. There's probably someone in the class who'd like to be friends and you haven't even noticed her.'

'Someone ugly like me.'

'Well, if that's your attitude.' She turned back to her desk. 'Why don't you smarten yourself up a bit? Comb your hair properly for a change, put on some of my pimple cream. Speak to them.'

Andrew waited at the top of the stairs. He looked into the glass of the painting opposite and tried to smooth his hair back over his ears. A couple of curls stuck out and he spat on his hand and pushed them down. They'd be along any minute now. All the girls from History. They'd come up the stairs and head along the top corridor to English. Laughing and swinging their bags. Hair shining, hanging over their shoulders and breasts. Boobs. Tits. He took out his comb and looked back at the painting. Sleepy cows, dreaming in golden paddocks. Storm brewing in purple and black clouds.

Hi, do you like the painting? (he could say). Or, did you finish that assignment on the writer of your choice? Or, did you watch 'Home and Away' last night? Voices. Shoes pounding on the stairs. Cass swung around the landing. Maria behind her and Cathy, Rodney, Pete, Jade. Others behind them.

Cass laughed. 'Making yourself bee-yoo-ti-ful? Hey, look, everyone, Andrew's making himself all beautiful.'

She was gone. Rodney ruffled Andrew's hair so that he dropped his comb. Then he too was gone, one hand on Cathy's back, and all the rest of them. Andrew was still standing. Kim was last. She picked up the comb and handed it to him without a word. He followed her along the corridor to the room where he sat alone in the chair closest to the door.

'How did you go today?' Anna stood, this time, in Andrew's doorway and watched as he spread the contents of his bag on his desk, his bed and the floor.

'What do you mean?'

'You know. The quest for a girlfriend.'

'No, I don't know what you mean.'

'Okay, okay. Don't get huffy. Did you talk to anyone today?'

'Not really.' He had shared computer time with Rebecca but Ms Rossi always said no talking unless it was to do with work and Rebecca never took her eyes off the screen.

'Being thirteen's a pain,' said Anna. 'One day it'll just all happen. Some princess'll kiss you and you'll turn into a handsome prince.'

'Piss off or I'll puke,' said Andrew.

He was late in to dinner. His father was spooning pasta and sauce from the bowls in the centre of the table. At the same time he was explaining something of great importance to Anna.

'What've you been doing?' asked his mother.

'Fossil stuff,' said Andrew. 'Did you know that, contrary to popular belief, the Jurassic wasn't the first stage of dinosaurs? They'd been around for ages and there were even amphibians two hundred million years before that.'

'. . . and,' Andrew's father put the bowl down, '. . . not only was he just the greatest, the greatest sax player ever, but he lived at a time when he was surrounded by greats. There's no question, jazz music has been going downhill ever since.' He sat down and twisted a scoop of spaghetti around his fork.

Anna looked at her mother. 'The men in this house are crazy. Loony. One's on about the Jazz age and the other's on about the Jurassic. What about the twentieth century? Or the twenty-first? We're almost there. I'm living in a house where one person is stuck eighty years ago and the other is stuck eight hundred million years ago.'

'Five hundred million,' said Andrew.

'What's the difference, five hundred million, eight hundred million.'

Andrew sucked up his pasta. 'It's the difference, der-brain, between an ammonite and a trilobite.'

'Sorry I asked.'

The next day he smoothed his hair down with water and a scoop of gel from the jar Anna kept beside the mouthwash and the tampons in the bathroom cupboard. He dabbed pimple cream on his chin and on a spot between his eyebrows. He caught the last morning bus, running down the hill in the warm sunlight. His shirt with the top two buttons undone and his school bag hanging off his left shouder. Only a few Year Twelve kids were there. They could wander into class whenever they liked. They didn't have to run for the second bell. He just made it and his shirt was hanging out now like a little kid.

'I want you to think about character,' said Ms Bell. 'As Drama students, character is the place we begin. When you take on a role, you need to know every little thing about the person you are. Outward things like what you look like, facial expressions, the way you walk.' She sat down on the edge of the desk and folded her arms. She didn't actually fold them; each hand cupped an elbow and held it as if she were posing. 'You also need to know the mind.' She waited for that to sink in. 'You need to understand feelings that then determine behaviour. So you have to work out every little thing about someone – favourite food, music, sports, movies. What they do in their spare time, who they are in love with or who they hate, what makes them laugh or cry. What in fact it is about them that makes them – them. If you know what I mean.'

She walked between the tables to the back of the room and spun round. An actor playing her part. 'An exercise in pairs. With your partner. Talk and find out as much as you can in five minutes. Make notes if you like. You want to know everything.'

Andrew was alone. Cass and Maria. Pete and Troy. Chris and Thomas. Rodney with Cathy. Kim.

'Andrew,' Ms Bell beckoned. 'Over here. Kim's on her own. Join her.' She moved away leaving no space for any protest. Andrew fell into the seat beside Kim.

'D'you want to go first?' she said.

'No. You.'

'Okay.' She doodled for a moment, eyes down towards the paper. Her jet-black fringe fell into her eyes. 'I don't know what to ask.'

They sat for a moment and then talk started all round the room and Kim wrote 'Andrew' at the top of her sheet and then put 'Height' underneath it.

'One hundred and forty-eight centimetres,' he said.

'Weight?' she asked.

He thought for a minute. On the scales that Anna threw

out when she became a born-again feminist, two months ago, he'd been forty-two kilos. That sounded like a primary-school kid. He calculated what sounded like a reasonable monthly addition, plus a bit more. 'Fifty kilos.'

'And what's your favourite sport?'

'Cricket. Football.' What would she say if he told her that he'd been no-balled six times in the last match of the summer playing in house cricket. No balls in football either. Not that he really cared. Scared shitless.

'What about music?' She wrote on the paper and looked up at him and almost smiled.

'The usual.' He leant his chair back and put his hands together, interlacing his fingers.

'What would that be?' she said. 'I don't listen to music much.'

'Oh? The Cure, Prince, not actually heavy metal.' He thought hard. I can't tell her it's all different in our house. When rock comes on the radio, Dad yells to me to turn that crap off. He plays blues in the pub on Friday nights while Mum sings and plays sax, and all week it's real old black musicians on scratchy recordings with names no one has heard of. Mum says they make your flesh crawl and your guts turn over. She reckons they'd eat Michael Jackson for breakfast.

'I don't actually know them,' confessed Kim. 'What makes you laugh? Cry? What do you do in your spare time?' She asked the questions and he answered, carefully choosing the replies that sounded bland and neatly packaged, able to have come from anyone. Answers that sit on styrofoam and are wrapped in plastic film.

I laugh at television soaps. I never cry at all and in my spare time I just muck around, you know, with mates and stuff, down at the pool, hang around the shopping centre, skating, go over to someone's place: just the usual. What would she say if I told her the truth?

'And who do you love?' said Kim.

That night, Andrew's mum and dad turned on their first summer barbecue. They were musos mainly and they stood on the back veranda, chewing blackened meat, onion and capsicum off little wooden sticks, talking of bands and gigs and pubs they'd played while Andrew organised their kids for a game of cricket. He didn't bowl, but stood near the fence ready to catch anything that looked like going over. Nothing did.

In my spare time I babysit a pile of little kids while their parents get pissed and talk themselves stupid.

'Andrew?' His mother came towards him. She was pulling a light cardigan around her shoulders. 'We're all going down to the pub to hear the last set. Anna wants to come with us. You'll keep an eye on the little ones, won't you?'

'Yeah.'

They went and Andrew took the kids inside and found an old video to put on for them. He fed them ice-cream and watched the movie with them for a while and then got bored and went off to his room to work with his collections.

In my spare time I collect fossils. I stick up pictures of dinosaurs in my room. I go to the museum and I look at fossils. I draw fossils. I hold rocks in my hands and move them a fraction till the light catches what's left after millions of years. I love fossils. That's what I'm in love with. Fossils.

He sat at his desk under the huge poster of Parasaurolophus and other dinosaurs of the Cretaceous period. Another poster showing the ages of the earth hung between the window and the bookcase. He picked up the rock in front of him and turned it over in his hands. It was an ordinary enough looking chunk of rock. Brownish reddish. But then the light caught it and you could see the outline of a beetle, or a beetle-like thing. Andrew picked up his pen and wrote on a card in front of him: 'Trilobite. Palaeozoic. Probably about five hundred million years old. Riversleigh. Queensland. 1992.' What would she have said if I'd told her I was into fossils? She'd tell the rest and the names would start again like primary school. Fossil. Dino the dinosaur. Tyro Tyrannosaurus. Not that I really minded. It was just boring.

She hadn't said much about what she liked.

'I'm one hundred and forty-two centimetres, forty kilos and I love Chinese food.'

'That's just as well,' said Andrew.

She had looked at him strangely when he'd said that.

'But I'm not Chinese,' she'd said so he'd gone on quickly with the next questions.

'I like all different sorts of music, going out, like to the movies and stuff like that.'

'What sort of movies?'

'Whatever's on. The usual.'

'Name one,' said Andrew. But she couldn't remember the last film she'd seen and had got a bit embarrassed and looked away.

Andrew put the rock back on the shelf and filed the card in the box on his desk. It was funny that she wouldn't answer that question directly. He stared at the long thin crest poking out of the head of Parasaurolophus that set it apart, made it so different from the others. What if. . . what if she was just the same as he was? What if she had a hobby, a life that was different from the others, if she felt outside it all, if she couldn't stand what they did and said and listened to and watched? What if she'd told him lies and covered up for herself the same way he had? Her own version of a fossil collection.

He was ready and eating breakfast when his mum came downstairs the next morning.

'You're early,' she said. 'Have you got a class before school?'

'Something like that.' He took his plate to the sink and washed the toast crumbs away. 'What time did you get back last night?'

'Late. We kicked on at Rod's place. Did the little ones behave themselves? They were asleep when we came in.'

'They were all right. I shoved a video on and then I went into my room.'

'More rocks?' said his mother.

'More rocks.' Andrew grinned and gave her his cheek to kiss. He stopped at the door. 'Mum, can I ask you something?'

'Please do. As long as it isn't about fossils.'

'What would you do if a class you were doing was all rubbish? It was just wrong what the teacher was saying?'

His mother poured coffee into a mug and swirled it around. 'I'd think very carefully about it. I'd make sure I knew what I was talking about and then I'd tell the teacher what I thought. Politely, though.' She looked up at him. 'Do you want to tell me more?'

'No, it's okay.'

He looked for Kim in the place under the trees where the Year Eight girls usually hung out. He could only see Cass and Maria and a few of the girls in classes that he didn't do. Kim wasn't in lines and he was already at his desk in Maths when she came in.

'Sorry I'm late,' she said to Ms Kelly who waved her to her seat in front of Andrew. He sat all lesson looking out the window or at the tiny gold circles she wore in her ears.

He fell into step with her on the way to Drama.

'Can I talk to you?'

'Sure, if you like,' she said. She was holding a pile of folders tight against her chest, talking over the top of them.

'It's sort of about what we were doing in Drama yesterday. You know, talking about all that stuff of what we're really like and what we do in our spare time and so on. Well, I just wanted to say that everything I told you was wrong. All lies. That's not what I'm like. I'm different from all that and I just thought. . .' Someone pushed past him. His folder fell to the floor. Papers scattered across the hall. He bent to pick them up. Kim knelt down, gathered up some papers and held them out to him.

'Tell me later,' she said. 'Everyone else has gone in.'

Again the lesson focussed on character.

'What did you learn?' said Ms Bell. Her bright red fingernails glowed from her crossed hands.

'We all know who Cathy's in love with,' said Cass.

'Shut up,' hissed Cathy.

Ms Bell raised an eyebrow. 'I did hope we could do exercises like this without this childishness. Peter. Tell us about Troy.'

'He's into sports and music. Summer it's cricket, winter it's soccer and basketball. He plays as well as watches. He doesn't like Michael Jackson or Prince or any of that. He reckons heavy metal's the best. Guns and Roses. He wants to go to concerts and gigs and stuff but sometimes he can't afford it or his mum and dad won't let him. They reckon he has to study and he knows that's sort of true but, like, he reckons you're only a kid once and you should enjoy your life before some stupid bastard blows the world up or runs over you or you have to get a job – or go on the dole, more likely.'

'Good.' Ms Bell drew the word out slowly as if she wasn't quite sure whether it was or not. 'What do you all think? Does that tell us something about Troy?'

'Mm.'

'Yeah.'

Andrew looked across the table to Kim. She was staring out the window, one hand playing with her gold earring. Light rain was falling. What Pete said was crap wrapped in plastic film. That told you nothing. Or not much. For all anyone knew, Troy could have a fossil collection too. Andrew started to chuckle.

'And what do you find so amusing?' Ms Bell stood up. She didn't look angry, just curious.

'Nothing.'

'This isn't kindergarten, Andrew. We share our thoughts here. I'm curious to know what you thought funny.'

Andrew took a deep breath. Kim was staring at him now. Dark-eyed. 'It's this whole exercise. I don't think it works.'

'Oh.' Ms Bell of the ironic eyebrow.

'Well, you can know a certain amount of stuff about somebody but that might tell you nothing of what they are really like. I mean, it's like dinosaurs.'

'Dinosaurs?'

'Yeah. You get a fossil which is one piece of information and you decide from that a whole lot of stuff. And then years later, someone finds another bone or something and you have to revise everything you thought. All your original projections might have been way off the track.'

'Apatosaurus and Brontosaurus,' said Ms Bell, almost under her breath.

'Yeah.' That threw him for a moment. How much did she know? 'And it's always guesswork.'

'Is that a reason not to do it?'

They were having the conversation entirely themselves, she sitting on her desk, him leaning forward, the rest of the class looking from one to the other. He didn't answer her directly.

'I mean,' he said, 'I could have told a whole lot of lies to Kim. She may not know any more about me than she did before we started.'

'True.' The teacher sat back. She nodded slowly. 'It could be that you construct a person, a character from the interview. Just the way that the actor constructs a character from the text. You interpret. It may not be the truth as your partner sees it, as the playwright saw it, but it is a valid interpretation from the evidence.'

'Just like a palaeontologist,' said Andrew.

'Just like a palaeontologist.'

Kim found Andrew in the study room during a free period. 'So is everything you told me a bunch of lies?'

Andrew looked up from his book. He hadn't been reading it. He had been watching the way Cathy and Rodney sat at the table by the window, their feet just brushing each other under the table. He had seen Kim come in and look around. He had been hoping she was looking for him.

He nodded. 'I thought you'd laugh or something, if I told you what I'm really like. I just told you all the stuff everyone else was telling. The truth is. . .'

'You don't have to tell me. You're not in class now.'

'I want to. Your Honour. The truth, the whole truth and nothing but the truth.'

She blushed a bit then. Andrew wasn't sure why. She sat down opposite him.

He began, 'I don't like football. I can't stand cricket. I think Michael Jackson sucks because he's a hypocrite and I wouldn't walk across the road to see The Cure. I don't hang around in shopping centres with mates 'cause I haven't got any, except Thomas sometimes. I haven't got any money either because anything I get is spent on fossils. I hang around the museum in their palaeontology department and in the next school holidays I'm going on a dig. Oh, and I'm not fifty kilos, I'm forty-six.' He sat back, breathless.

She grinned at him across the folders. 'And who do you love?' she said. They both laughed.

Maria came in at that moment to check the assignment sheet for History. 'What's so funny?' She sat down.

'Private joke,' said Kim.

Andrew got up and left. He heard Maria, as he walked across to the library computer. 'I didn't know you had a thing for him?'

When Andrew got home, Anna was in the kitchen heating up soup.

'Hi,' she said. 'Mum and Dad have gone to a meeting. I'm going over to Rick's place to study. Mum said to help yourself to some food.' She sipped the reddish liquid from the spoon. 'As if you need any encouragement. They'll be home about ten.'

After she'd gone, Andrew sat in the kitchen slurping soup from a bowl. He watched the afternoon shadows spread across the yard. The cat was stalking cockroaches along the back of the barbecue. A white plastic bag blew over the brick wall from next door. He sat there till it was almost dark.

The phone rang. He let it ring a few times. It would be for Anna. He had homework to do: Maths problems, a work sheet for History. He could bring it into the kitchen table. He picked up the phone.

'560 6419'

'Oh. . . I. . . um. . . is that Andrew?'

'Yes.'

'Oh. . . I wasn't sure if this would be the right number.'

Now *he* wasn't sure. 'Who's speaking?'

'It's Kim. From school. '

'Kim.'

There was silence on the other end.

'Are you still there, Kim?'

'Yes.'

'For a minute I thought you'd hung up.'

'I will if you want me to.'

'No, no. I just wasn't expecting to hear from you. That's all.'

'You sure?'

'Sure I'm sure.'

They both laughed and then there was silence again.

'I. . .'

'I. . .'

They laughed together again.

'You first,' said Andrew.

'Well,' said Kim. 'I was just ringing to say that I was sorry that Maria interrupted us at study time. I didn't want her to stay.'

'I was going to say the same thing. I was sorry too.'

'And then I looked for you after school,' said Kim. 'But you must have got away pretty quickly.'

'I went up to the library. I had some books to get back. They were overdue.'

'I sometimes go up there to study,' said Kim. 'Gets a bit noisy round our place sometimes.'

'Yeah, it's pretty good up there. Librarian's okay.'

'Yeah. I like the way she really helps you and lets you use the photocopier and everything.'

'Yeah.'

Andrew sat, cross legged, under the lounge-room window. He lifted the phone from the table and put it beside him and leant back against the wall. He had never sat talking on the phone like this before.

Kim asked him about Maths homework and what he thought of Ms Kelly. He asked her what she was writing about in the English essay and if she'd finished reading the novel yet.

Then she said, 'How come you never bring your fossils to school?'

'No way. They might get damaged and no one in our class would be interested.'

'How do you know if you haven't tried them? Anyway, can I come and have a look one day?'

'Sure. *You* can.'

After a pause, Kim said, 'I was wondering if you were going to Fran's party.'

'No.'

'How come?'

'Wasn't invited. Are you going?'

'Yeah,' said Kim. 'Fran's sort of my best friend lately. I never used to hang round with her. She was so quiet when she first came. I'll fix it with her. . . if you want to come.'

'Yeah. Be great.'

There was another pause and then Andrew spoke. 'Kim, you know how I said I told you all that stuff that was wrong. Well, I. . . I sort of thought that you maybe had things you were interested in that you hadn't told anyone either.'

'Like a fossil collection.'

'It's sort of what I mean.'

There was a pause on the other end, then muffled voices.

'I've got to go now,' said Kim. 'That was Mum. I told her I was checking homework and she says we've been nearly half an hour already. I'll answer your question another time. Okay?'

'Okay. See you tomorrow.'

She hung up and he went and got his books and sat down at the kitchen table. The Maths problems were easy. He finished them and then went into the lounge room to put on some music. He flicked through the drawer full of records, CDs and tapes. Louis Armstrong, Bo Diddley, Ella Fitzgerald. . . Mahalia Jackson. Michael's grandma maybe? He laughed. He couldn't remember her. His mother's favourite Billie Halliday album was on top of the cabinet. He took the old vinyl record out of its sleeve and wiped off the dust. He turned the lights down, switched on the record player and watched as the arm lifted across and dropped onto the black circle. The music came, slow and reedy. Clarinet maybe with piano behind it. Then trumpet and saxophone. Like Mum's, only better. Through the scratches came the high lonely voice. Love and losing. Sadness. Sorrow. Love and gaining again and again.

He started to move. Slowly at first, his bare feet pressing into the soft carpet. He swayed and then took small steps, his upper body still while he rolled his hips and went forward, then back and to the side. He closed his eyes and rolled his shoulders. He crooned and moved and love thoughts oozed from his mind, along his spine through to his hands, to his thighs and to his feet and the whole of his body.

Is this what Mum meant?

He had never felt and sung and danced this way before.

I am the dinosaur and the one in search of it. Each piece of me I find tells me more. It adds and changes. Who knows what else there is? Of me? Of her? When she answers. When I see her. Tomorrow.

CATHY AND RODNEY

'Mum's had a go at me about Rodney.' Cathy stretched out on her towel, her long tanned legs gleaming with drops of water. Cass and Maria and Rebecca looked up. Red and green noses and shoulders. Hot sun. Splashing and shouts from the pool.

'How come?'

'I was late again last night. We were just doing some homework and we watched a video. His mum and dad were there. When I got back she was waiting up and she pulled this really heavy voice.' Cathy laughed and sat up and frowned in imitation. 'I need to talk to you, young lady. In the morning.' She wagged her finger, put her hands on her hips and cocked her head to one side. Then she rolled onto her back and looked up at the jacaranda, purple against the blue sky. 'After breakfast I got the lot. It wasn't about last night. More about us getting too serious. She thinks we're doing it. She'd be happier if we broke up, or I joined a nunnery. She'll calm down in the end.'

That morning, her mother had stood at the sink. Her gardening shorts were frayed around the hem and had grass and dirt stains. A back pocket hung by a few threads. She had brushed some long grey strands of hair back from her cheek and gone on sorting flowers from the garden into piles of different length and colour. She had snipped the extra leaves off roses, geraniums and grevillea. Then she'd bashed the ends of the stalks with the meat tenderiser. Slivers of green splattered over the bread board. 'They'll last longer,' she'd said. And then, 'I'm worried about you and Rodney.' Snip, snip. 'He's a nice boy and, through the year, I've got to quite like him, but you're getting too serious. You should be going out with lots of boys. We all went out in groups when we were your age.' Bash, bash. 'You're attractive. You could go out with whoever you like. Don't tie yourself down.'

'We're not getting married.' Cathy was trapped. She couldn't leave the room. She couldn't look at her mother. She'd picked up a purple felt pen and scribbled on the calendar hanging beside the window. Wilderness Society. Wild stream cascading over green moss-covered rocks. Doodles of letters, R and C.

'I should think not. You're fourteen, Cathy. You've got your whole life ahead of you.' She'd wiped her hands and sat down at the table and spoken more quietly. 'Look, love. You get serious with one boy too soon and the temptation is to get too involved, too intimate. . .'

'You mean sex?'

'Yes. I do mean sex. You know all the mechanics. You kids are far better informed than we were. But it's about relationships. It's more complicated than that and you're too young for that complication.'

'It's so boring.' Cathy took a bag of apricots out of her bag and put them in front of her. 'Groups, groups, groups. It's all she ever talks about.' She sat up cross legged and sucked on the fleshy golden fruit. 'I keep telling her that it's not really serious, we aren't actually doing it, and that we do go out in the group. She wouldn't know the difference.' She tossed her long hair back and rolled her eyes. 'I wonder if she'd be any happier if I went out with a different guy every week?'

'Then she'd think you were a nymphomaniac,' said Cass.

'A nympho – what?' said Maria.

'Forget it.'

'You could try someone in Year Nine.'

'Or that hunk who was at skating Friday night.'

'Which one?'

'Don't act like you didn't notice,' said Cass. 'Black ponytail. Three silver earrings and two girls from Year Ten.' She took an apricot from the bag, ate it and then kept sucking the stone, rolling it round her mouth. 'My mum's always going on about groups too. Do you think they used to do stuff at parties, like, you know, kissing and um, you know. . .?'

'Do you think they used to have parties?'

'I think they were all virgins till they got married.'

'I think they still are.'

'Don't be stupid.' Rebecca sat up. 'Where do you think you came from?'

'Stork.'

'Cabbage leaf.'

'The fairies.'

'Immaculate conception.' Maria smirked.

'You sound like a Catholic.'

Cathy and Rebecca went to swim laps. Maria and Cass lay on their towels, heads resting on their arms, the hot sun on their backs.

'I'm baby-sitting tonight,' said Maria. 'I didn't think Dad'd let me but Mum talked him into it. Next door. He's just gorgeous. Two months old and smiling already. He's got all this really cute curly black hair. He takes his bottle from me.' She looked up. 'You're not even listening.'

'Sorry,' said Cass. 'I was thinking about Cathy and Rodney. What d'you reckon's going on?'

'What do you mean?'

Cass frowned. 'That's not the first time that she's been going on about what her mum says. I wonder. . .' She pushed herself up on her elbows. 'It could be like that video we watched at your place last weekend. Remember how that guy kept saying how the old bloke looked really sick when he wasn't and then he bumped him off and no one suspected that it was murder?'

'Are you saying that Cathy is going to murder Rodney?'

'Course not. I reckon she's planning to give him the flick and she's going to say that her mum made her when really it's what she wants herself.'

'You've got an overactive imagination.'

'All this going on about groups. She's planning something. I reckon she's keen on someone a bit older and she's going to see if she can get him.'

'D'you really think so?'

'I'll bet you.'

Maria ran into Fran in the video shop.

'Did you know Cathy's thinking of dropping Rodney?'

'No kidding?'

'She told us this afternoon. Well. Sort of. Her mum's making her. But she's got her eye on someone else.'

On the phone later that night, Fran told Kim. 'Cathy's dropping Rodney. I'm surprised you didn't know. Everyone else does.

We think she's got this older guy. He's supposed to be really good-looking.'

'When did this happen?'

'This weekend, I think.'

Kim rang Andrew. 'You didn't tell me that Cathy and Rodney had broken up.'

'I didn't know.'

Andrew ran into Rodney at the bus stop on the way to school, on Monday.

'Bit of a bummer about you and Cathy, mate,' he said.

Cathy meets me, most days, as soon as I get to school. She comes across the playground, bag slung over her shoulder. Big grin. She says 'Gidday' and touches my arm and looks at me. She just looks at me and everything's great. But not that day.

What did Andrew mean? What was he talking about? She hadn't rung last night – true, I'd been out at the Pizza Place with Dad, but she usually leaves me messages and I ring her back.

I looked for her when I got to school. Cass and Maria and Rebecca were in their usual spot under the trees. I started to walk towards them and Cass whispered something to Maria and I just knew it was about me. I felt cold then. Like before a big race, the moment when you're all tensed and all you can see is the water and all you listen for is the gun. I changed direction. I didn't even sidestep, just a bit of a swerve as if I really was headed for the canteen all the time. I hung out there with the chip eaters and the Coke guzzlers till lines and then I couldn't avoid them.

'Where's Cathy?' I whispered to Cass.

'Dentist.'

Why hadn't she told me? But what did Andrew mean?

Next thing, we're in Science. Experiment time and Pete leant across the benches and he said, 'So what's up with you and Cathy?'

'Nothing.' I didn't take my eyes off the flame from the bunsen burner. My hand on the control switch was shaking.

'Not what I heard,' he said.

Stay cool. Act like you know but you're not saying. 'And what did you hear?' I said.

'That she's got some other guy from Year Nine or skating or something.'

'Who told you?'

'Thomas.'

I could see Thomas in the front row, head bent over his experiment. Rebecca too. Brain rubbing again after all that shit in Canberra. Wouldn't catch me doing that. Not if someone said that about me. Thick as anything after they won that prize. I gave Pete my notes and I barged up the front. I stood in front of him so he had to notice. 'Hey, Thomas, who told you Cathy and me had broken up?' He looked at Rebecca and then back at me. He shrugged and squirmed a bit. I'm lots bigger than he is.

'I don't know. Sorry, mate. Everyone's talking about it.'

Everyone except me.

I kicked Troy's bag on the way back to my seat. He swore. I said a few things back and Mr Carantinos came out of the preparation room. He said some stuff that I can't remember. I mumbled something. How could she have broken it off without telling me? That was what you did at primary school. Not when you were just about adults. Doing what we did. Touching. And all that. My hands were sweat rags.

I drifted through Science and then English like I was stoned or something. Everyone left me alone. Rejected lover. Rejected. Dejected. I ignored Thomas when he went to sit next to me and he soon got the message and sat further up the back.

Ms Bell started handing back Drama assignments and went on and on about the two main characters in the play. 'Relationships,' she said. 'I wanted analysis of the relationship, not some old crib note about the colour of eyes or length of hair. I wanted feelings. I wanted to know what was going on between these two people.'

'I'm going to be sick,' I said 'I'm going to chuck.' I just about ran all the way down the stairs. It was hot out in the playground. I didn't know whether to head off home, or go up the street or what. I sat down under the big trees. It's where the girls always sit at lunch time. They all go there like it's their special place and no one else ever takes it.

It was like I was sitting in her seat. I could almost smell the way her hair smells when she washes it and leaves it out all over her shoulders and down her back. I could feel the way her skin feels. At the pool we lie and let our feet rub together and I put my arm across her back and let my fingers follow the softness down her side. She strokes my shoulder, kisses me on the neck, on my cheek and my ear.

How could she break it off and not tell me?

When I was eight I had this little rabbit and one day it got out of its cage and it got run over. Squashed on the hot summer bitumen outside. Mum found it and the flies and the smell and she scraped it off the road and she buried it and didn't tell me until afterwards. I wished I'd been there, when it happened. Just so I knew it was true.

'Rodney.' Her voice calling my name. I felt like some dumb dork in the movies, wishing for her and then there she is. But it was her. Coming through the gates, hair swinging, smiling at me as if nothing had changed. 'What are you doing out of class?' One hand stretched out to touch my arm.

I pulled away. 'Where have you been?'

'The dentist.' She frowned and stepped back. 'But what about you?'

'I didn't feel too good.'

'What's wrong?'

'You ought to know.' I was on my feet, out of the cool shade. Sun and glare off the brick walls. My body burned under the thin cotton shirt. It burned to have her touch me. Kiss me.

She frowned. I felt a stinging behind my eyes. Don't cry. For chrissake don't cry. I turned away from her.

The bell went then and kids started to pour out of the doors of the library and the main block.

'Rodney,' she called. I wanted to turn back. Forget the morning. Forget what they were saying. Put my arms around her like always, hold her close.

'Rodney.'

But I didn't. I was sick in my guts. I ran from her. Straight into the boys' toilet, opened the first door and chucked into the bowl.

~

He was in our place, under the trees. He looked sick, shoulders hunched like a little kid on his own on his first day.

I went up to him just like I always do, and I was going to touch him, maybe even sneak a kiss, school playground and all, but he leapt up and then pulled away from me as if I was a stranger or an enemy or something. Weird as hell. I asked him what was going on. He just didn't look like the same person. I mean we've been going out together for months. I know him. But he kept looking at me like I had the plague and then he ran off to the boys' toilets. Left me standing. Everyone was coming out by then. I went up to Pete to see if he knew what was going on and he just gave me a dirty look and said I ought to know.

'Ought to know what?' I said. 'What's going on?'

'That you two are broken up. Finito. Nice one, Cathy. He's had enough.'

I left then.

I went up the street, by the back lane. You get sprung on the main road. Rubbish stinks. I hardly noticed. What did Pete mean? What am I supposed to know? Has Rodney broken it off? We were okay on Friday. He's not usually moody. We've never argued, not that I remember. Nice one, Cathy. Why? Carol? He's always said he'd never go back to her. And she's got someone outside school. How dare he? I kicked this pile of junk, lettuce leaves and rotten fruit so it smashed on a back fence and the next minute I just wanted to run home and curl up on the doona on my bed and cry.

I came out between the library and the Greek church. An old woman in black was standing near the door. She was so tiny she reminded me of Nana Pearson when she died and I was only ten and that made me want to cry all over again. She watched me go into the cafe. I sat under the Capri posters where Rodney and I always sit. We go there when Mum thinks we're doing research on assignments. I ordered my usual caramel milkshake. Con looked like he was going to ask me what I was doing there at that hour of the morning but he didn't. I sucked the straw, staring at the weird patterns in the yellow laminex table top. He'd sit opposite. Our ankles'd touch. We'd hold hands. Looking, just looking at each other.

~~~

I stayed in the toilets till everyone had gone back to class. Chucking made me feel shivery and empty. Pete and the others were like vultures circling over a corpse, wasps on a squashed jam sandwich, ants crawling on a dead Christmas beetle. I wasn't angry any more. Just sick and on my own.

~~~

Cass rang me.

'Listen, Cathy,' she said. She often starts like that. Of course I'm listening. I'm holding the phone, aren't I?

'We reckon,' she said, 'that you've done the right thing.'

What had I done? I didn't have the energy to ask. I felt so tired that I wanted to hang up and slip down onto the floor and go to sleep.

'Are you still there, Cath?'

'Yeah. I'm still here.'

'What are you going to do now?'

'Have dinner,' I said. That's not what she wanted to hear. She wanted details. Gory ones. She always does. But I didn't have any to give. I didn't know what was going on.

Rebecca rang then. She said it was just to see if I was okay. She's nice like that. I said I was fine and then she went on about how she and Thomas had got back together after Canberra and after they'd done so well in the Maths competition and how it would be the same for us. How can she say it's the same? They weren't even together before Canberra. Not really. Brain rubbing Rodney calls it, whereas we. . . He said that on one of those cold nights in Canberra. 'We rub other bits,' he said and grinned and his hands were inside my shirt, warming my skin, my back, my. . . I couldn't stand thinking about it. I wanted to phone him, ask him why, what's going on? I even picked up the phone and tried to dial the number. But I couldn't.

Pete and Troy came round after school. If I'd been quick I'd've told them I was too sick to see anyone. Chickenpox or plague. We sat around in the kitchen and talked about nothing. I couldn't eat but they knocked off the leftover pie from the night before and a whole litre of milk.

'You're better off without her. Stuck-up bitch,' Troy said.

Jealous bastard. The only kisses he's ever had are from his mother and grandmother.

'I wouldn't even talk to her, if I was you,' said Pete. 'You can have whoever you like.'

She was who I liked.

Lovesick women are supposed to starve themselves but I was hungry. I didn't tell Mum. She'd had some meeting at work and she was pretty tired. Dad was out so it was just the two of us eating takeaway.We had a cold chicken, picnic style and

I tore the bits off and licked the juice that dripped from my fingers.

She talked on and on about this problem she was having. She runs this lab and she's not getting on with one of her technicians and she's trying to solve it by sitting down and talking and talking to him. All this stuff about working problems through and not getting to the point where you yell at each other and walk away. Most appropriate. Ha ha. If she only knew.

'You're quiet,' she said. 'Is something up?'

I didn't mean to tell her but it all just came out. I told her how I didn't know how it happened but everyone was talking as if we were broken up and he was acting weird and I didn't know what was going on. I thought she'd be pleased, and I told her so, but she pulled her chair up close to mine and she said how sorry she was that I was unhappy but that was all part of it, and she rubbed my back and my neck just like she used to when I'd fallen down and hurt myself when I was a little girl.

I was glad when Pete and Troy left. I went and lay on the grass out the back. Our dopey dog came and licked my face and flopped across my feet and I left him there. It was hot but it was sort of comfortable. I'd been bored in the kitchen. I didn't want to sit around talking with them. Cathy. Where was she? What was she doing? What was she thinking? I stayed there on the grass for ages, going round and round in circles. What for? What if? Why? Dad came home and called me in and I washed lettuce and cut tomatoes while he made a stir-fry.

'How's things?' he said.

'Like shit.'

'Quit the swearing. What's up? Had a fight with Cath?'

'And the rest.'

'She'll get over it.'

'It's not like that.'

'Did she give you the big heave-ho?'

'I think so.'

'Listen, mate. Either she did or she didn't.'

So I told him. It sounded weird, like it had happened to someone else. I didn't ask him what he reckoned I should do and he didn't tell me, but he did go on a bit about relationships – that bloody word again – being hard work and you have to talk about them all the time.

I wasn't listening all that much. I kept imagining her coming back. Like I'd be walking into school and she'd be waiting for me and she'd say it was all a crazy mistake and could we get back on together. Or she'd be really sick and her mum would ring me and beg me to go over there because only seeing me would make her well again. Crazy dream stuff. Fairytale.

~~~

Mum came in and kissed me goodnight. She never does that. Usually she blows me one as I walk out the lounge room. Made me feel a bit bad for all the times I'd said I was going over to Cass's place when really I was off to somewhere with Rodney. Damn Rodney. I lay still. Frozen. I heard the tiniest creak in the floorboards, the brushing of a branch against the side of the house, the engine of a car at the corner, three blocks away. I felt the weight of the cool sheet on my bare skin. Weird
~~~

thoughts. Him in danger, burning building, runaway horse, floodwaters. I come to the rescue. Superwoman. Cool, powerful. He begs to come back to me. I take him in. I fight a duel for him. I win but am wounded and he bathes my body, soothing my wounds with ointments, touch and kisses.

I fell asleep curled up like a baby.

~

Dad and Mum both went to work early. I didn't want to go to school. I couldn't face all the looks and questions. Pete banged on the door on his way past but I stuck my head out of the upstairs window and told him I was sick and I wasn't coming. I didn't feel sick. Not angry either any more. Just like a hollow tree, the sap all sucked out. I stayed in bed for ages and then when it got really hot I decided to get up and go to the pool. No one's there in the middle of the day except a few mothers and little kids. No distractions. No screaming, no splashing. I had this thought that I would dive in one end and I'd swim laps till I couldn't swim any further.

~

'Why don't you have a day off?' Mum said when she left for work. 'Your exams are over. One day won't hurt.' She looked all concerned and if it wasn't for the heat she'd've got me a hot-water bottle and tucked me up with a warm drink. It wouldn't last but I liked it. Then Dad poked his head around the door and told me to look after myself. I went back to sleep for a while and then I got up and mooched around for a bit. It was stinking hot outside, the first one like it this summer, the sort of day that melts you. Sweat in your hair and eyes and trickling down your legs. I wrapped myself in a sarong. Too hot to read. Too hot to eat . Nothing on television. I wasn't angry any more. I decided that what I did want to do was cool off and I took my costume and towel and went to the pool.

~~~

I was up to twenty lengths before I started to feel tired. Cathy kept coming into my head and I kept pushing her out. Her face, her smile, her eyes. I started saying Science homework. The order of planets from the Sun: Mercury, Venus, Earth, Mars. . . The feel of her body brushing up to me on the stairs or in the library. I started to sing the words of songs. Trouble was, they were usually about love and losing and I didn't need that. Finally I just counted strokes. Long slow overarm like a coach I had in primary school once taught me. There was hardly anyone else there. A couple of little kids in the shallow end and an old man cooling off in the middle. When I got to twenty-five laps I noticed another swimmer in the far lane but she was too far away to bother me.

~~~

The pool was nearly empty. There was only this one guy doing laps, some little kids down the end and an old bloke dog paddling in a circle in the middle. I got in near the wall to avoid the waves that the other swimmer was making. I like doing laps. I trained a lot in primary school. Sometimes Mum and I go in the morning and work up an appetite before breakfast. When the other kids are there in the afternoon and at the weekends we always muck around and have a good time and there's not much chance to do anything like that.

I don't know what it is. It's not like when I go skating, racing about with your hair flying and other people trying to keep up, the air on your face. But there's something about being on your own. Sometimes I think about all sorts of stuff, arguments I've had, conversations and what I should've said. Other times it's like the water washes your brain out.

This time, Rodney kept coming in. Not the bits that had just happened. That was a blur. But odd things. The look on his face that night of my party, it seems ages ago now, when Dad found him in my room and we weren't doing anything but Dad wouldn't listen. The crazy card he drew me for my birthday. The way he held my little finger in the cafe under the posters of Capri. I tried to push them out. I swam faster and faster. Concentrate on strokes. One breath every four, every six arm movements. It was as if the faster I went the more I could push the sadness away.

I had moved away from the wall, into the next lane. The other swimmer had moved a bit towards me. We were in adjoining lanes, him on my blind side, but a fair way ahead. I was moving up on him. Dark shadow. The wash from his kicking lapped around my face. I started to pull my arms harder, to kick more strongly. I had this need to catch and pass him and go on. Like a district carnival race. I held my breath for six and then eight strokes. Kick. Pull. Kick. Pull. Kick. Pull. No audience, no crowd, no cheering. Just me. My breathing got quicker. My face was level with his knees. My chest hurt. He seemed to go faster. Did he feel me there? I was level with his thighs, his waist. Our arms moved together, legs together, bodies together. Slapping the water. Kick. Pull. Breathing in time. We hurled ourselves at the wall.

~~~
~~~

Cathy. Rodney.

Gasping. Holding the wall. Shoulders heave. Eyes wide.

'Why aren't you. . .?'

'What are you. . .?'

Laughing. Hands reached across the bobbing yellow cork of the lane-dividing rope. Fingers touched, slid along arms. We moved towards each other. The rope cut into our skin.

'I missed you.'

'Me too.'

Lips wet.

'I'll come under.'

'No, I will.'

We duckdived and met on the bottom. We held each other, rolling and rolling. Legs entwined. Together. Gently floating to the surface.

ABOUT THE AUTHOR

Libby Gleeson was born in New South Wales, one of six children. After studying history at Sydney University, she spent five years in Italy and London. On returning home she first taught in high schools, then in adult education. Now she is a full-time writer and lives with her husband and three daughters in Sydney.

Her first novel for young readers, *Eleanor, Elizabeth*, was the winner of the Angus & Robertson Writers for the Young Fellowship and was Highly Commended in the 1985 Children's Book Council of Australia Book of the Year Awards. Her second novel, *I am Susannah*, was a 1988 Honour Book in the same awards, and her third novel, *Dodger*, won the 1991 Australian Children's Literature Peace Prize and an IBBY (International Board of Books for Young People) Award.

Libby is also the author of several picture books, including *Where's Mum?*, illustrated by Craig Smith and shortlisted for the 1993 Children's Book Council of Australia Picture Book of the Year Award.

MORE GREAT READING FROM PUFFIN

☆☆☆☆☆☆☆☆☆☆☆☆☆☆☆☆☆☆☆☆☆☆☆☆☆☆☆☆☆☆☆☆

Eleanor, Elizabeth Libby Gleeson

Eleanor has had to leave the town she grew up in, but her new home holds many secrets to be uncovered, secrets of her mother's childhood and of her grandmother, Elizabeth.

Highly Commended in the 1984 Australian Children's Book of the Year Awards.

The House that was Eureka Nadia Wheatley

When Evie, Noel and Noel's grandmother come together in adjoining terrace houses in Sydney's inner city, something more powerful than a dream sets the past back in motion.

Winner of the 1986 NSW Premier's Award for Literature. Commended in the 1986 Australian Children's Book of the Year Awards. Shortlisted for the SA Premier's Award.

Megan's Star Allan Baillie

Kel has rare powers and knows that Megan has them too. But as they explore their capabilities, Megan realises she must soon give up all she knows, for there will be no turning back.

Shortlisted for the 1989 Australian Children's Book of the Year Award and the 1989 NSW Premier's Award.

MORE GREAT READING FROM PUFFIN

☆☆☆☆☆☆☆☆☆☆☆☆☆☆☆☆☆☆☆☆☆☆☆☆☆☆☆☆☆☆

Games . . . Robin Klein

When Patricia is invited to a party by Kirsty and Genevieve she can't believe her luck. But the planned party falls through and soon Kirsty's spiteful games are out of control and the girls are plunged into a night of terror.

The White Guinea Pig Ursula Dubosarsky

When Geraldine is entrusted with the care of her friend's white guinea pig, Alberta, and when that guinea pig mysteriously disappears, it is the beginning of Geraldine's growing up, and everything in her life changes.

Spider Mansion Caroline Macdonald

What happens when your pleasant, easy-going guests gradually appear to be something else entirely? This psychological thriller has its characters enmeshed in a spiralling web of fear.

MORE GREAT READING FROM PUFFIN

☆☆☆☆☆☆☆☆☆☆☆☆☆☆☆☆☆☆☆☆☆☆☆☆☆☆☆☆☆☆☆☆☆☆☆

Ganglands Maureen McCarthy

The dramatic story of the summer when Kelly leaves school – when she will be faced with the toughest decisions of her life. Set in the cultural melting-pot of inner-city Melbourne, from the author of the *In Between* series.

Galax-Arena Gillian Rubinstein

What is it like to be a pet of another species? Is it better to risk your life for an alien audience, or starve to death in your own land? If you were offered safety in exchange for selling others into slavery, would you take it?

Named an Honour Book in the 1993 Children's Book Council of Australia Book of the Year Awards for older readers.

The Gathering Isobelle Carmody

Nathanial comes to Cheshunt unwillingly. Before long he discovers that Cheshunt is a town with a dark secret; an ancient evil which he and four others must confront. Together they must find a way to defeat the Gathering and its master.

Joint winner of the 1993 Children's Peace Literature Award.

MORE GREAT READING FROM PUFFIN

☆☆☆☆☆☆☆☆☆☆☆☆☆☆☆☆☆☆☆☆☆☆☆☆☆☆☆☆☆☆

Goodbye and Hello Clodagh Corcoran/Margot Tyrrell (Eds)

An innovative anthology of sixteen stories by Irish and Australian writers in which everyone is coming to terms with a goodbye or a hello. An exciting new collection for older readers.

Landmarks Nadia Wheatley (Ed)

Nine new stories by top Australian authors. Set against a variety of rural and urban landscapes, these stories explore the turning points in the lives of very different young people.

Tearaways Robin Klein

They're different, unpredictable . . . They're tearaways, and they're dangerous. These razor-sharp stories from this brilliant writer will make you think twice.

A Children's Book Council of Australia Notable Book, 1991.

MORE GREAT READING FROM PUFFIN

☆☆☆☆☆☆☆☆☆☆☆☆☆☆☆☆☆☆☆☆☆☆☆☆☆☆☆☆☆☆☆☆☆☆☆☆☆

Lovebird Peter McFarlane

From the author of *The Flea and Other Stories* here is a powerful new collection of unforgettable characters.

Kissing the Toad Doug MacLeod (Ed)

An anthology of stories and poems by young Australian writers, chosen from entrants in the *International Youth Year Australian Young Writers' Project.*

Bittersweet Toss Gascoigne (Ed)

Stories about love, relationships and heartache from Australia's most popular and award-winning authors.